Strange Loop

The Cabalist

Conversations with Lord Byron
on Perversion, 163 Years After
His Lordship's Death

The Side of the MOON

AMANDA PRANTERA

BLOOMSBURY

First published in Great Britain 1991

Copyright © 1991 by Amanda Prantera

The moral right of the author has been asserted

Bloomsbury Publishing Ltd, 2 Soho Square, London W1V 5DE

A CIP catalogue record for this book
is available from the British Library

ISBN 0 7475 0861 5

10 9 8 7 6 5 4 3 2 1

Typeset by Hewer Text Composition Services, Edinburgh
Printed in Great Britain by Butler & Tanner Ltd, Frome and London

For Cosimo
Mihi maxima res sub caelo

THE SIDE OF THE MOON

AUTHOR'S NOTE

To me of course everything in this book is true in some sense of that enigmatic word, otherwise I would hardly have dared write it, let alone ask other people to read it. If anyone wants to work out for themselves, however, what is true in the more canonical sense, then the following bits of information may come in handy.

GALEN, the narrator, was born in Pergamos in Asia Minor in the year A.D. 130 *circa*, and is telling his story in Rome at the self-confessed age of nearly seventy, under the rule of Septimius Severus. This means we are in the heart of the already declining Roman Empire in the year A.D. 199 or thereabouts. Despite the fact that twenty-two volumes of Galen's work managed to escape fire and other hazards and have come down to us, we know little about him as a man, save that he was immensely famous in his time and for over a thousand years afterwards, that he had a shrewish mother who bit her maids, and that he was personal doctor to the Emperor Marcus Aurelius and to Marcus Aurelius's son Commodus. To those who would know more I recommend the above books, but warn that of the twenty-two only one is regularly translated from the ancient Greek, and even that is rather tough going.

CASSIUS DIO COCCEIANUS, Galen's listener, was born in Bithynia, Asia Minor, in A.D. 163 and died there in 235. In time off from public service he eventually fulfilled his literary ambition and wrote a vast history of what he called 'Roman Affairs', covering everything from the birth of the Republic down to his own day and filling eighty volumes. Several of these survive, some intact, some heavily abridged and patched together by later historians. Books LXXI to LXXV are the ones which reflect Galen's story although not perhaps quite as fully or faithfully as the Galen of this book would have liked. Given their age and the accidents that have befallen them, they still make surprisingly chatty and interesting reading.

Galen's story turns around four main characters: the Emperor Marcus Aurelius, his wife Faustina, his son Commodus, and his adopted

daughter Marcia. Of these four only MARCUS AURELIUS himself
(A.D. 121–180) leaves behind him writings: namely a delightful batch
of letters and the much discussed Journal or Daybook of the text,
which is of course published nowadays under the more usual title of
Meditations or sometimes *Thoughts of Marcus Aurelius.* This is one of the
world's greatest books and needs no promotion from me, but if
anyone has missed out on it, or like me only read bits of it as a child at
school, then I urge them, as I did myself, to go back and read the
whole; not for any weight that it lends to my own hypothesis, which is
very little really, but just for the sheer beauty of it.

PART I

EXECUTION AND SENTENCE

ETIAM PERIERE RUINÆ

(A phrase used by Lucan of the razing of Troy
to imply a job well done: Even the ruins were
destroyed.)

Failure comes to most men but to most men it has the grace to
come gently: it creeps in through the back door like a cat, curls
itself up in a corner, and is careful to call no attention to itself until
it has been accepted as part of the household. By which time it will
be seen to be a snug, companionable beast, not what it is made out
to be at all, and quite unworth the trouble of chasing away.

To me, however, failure came differently, not like a cat but like
a lioness – padding silently along behind unnoticed and then giving
one deft, fell spring to the neck. And in this I was perhaps fortunate,
for no one likes to keep a bounding great lioness in the vicinity for
very long; the urge is more to repel it.

I ought, of course, had my political nose been anything like
my medical one, to have sensed the animal's approach earlier. Four
months earlier to be precise, when the great fire broke out in the
Archives, destroying not only the pertinent section of my own writings and all the notes and documents on which they were based,
but the entire corpus of the Records of State for the past thirty and
more years. The smell of that particular conflagration, if nothing else,
should have put me on the alert.

But alas it did not, my nose was what it was, my ties with the Court
had grown slacker by then (entirely my own doing, I may add: it was
and always had been an essential part of the plan that with the passing
of the years I should fade more and more into the background), and
time and habit had evidently made me complacent. Things had not
gone smoothly, but they had gone. The worst of the obstacles had
been surmounted. There was as yet no heir, of course, nothing but a
string of early miscarriages, but there was – or appeared to be – plenty
of time, still, in which if not to fashion then to procure one. There was
no enthusiastic support from the families of the old aristocracy for

the new regime, and this was only to be expected, but there was – or again appeared to be – a kind of stunned acceptance which for practical purposes came to much the same thing. Who cared why these people were quiet, I mean, as long as they were quiet? I knew the Emperor was still having difficulties, particularly over his tax-levy reform; I knew he had more enemies than hairs on his head but reckoned they were dwindling at much the same speed; I knew that he had fought the fire in the Archives with his own hands and was said to bear the marks of the burns on them. I had even heard that he had temporarily transferred his sleeping quarters to the secluded old villa on the Caelian hill (never a good sign when a man in time of trouble goes back to a childhood retreat – it smacks of tail-biting, finality, a closing of the circle), but none of this added up in my mind to yield the simple sum that his downfall was imminent.

Thus the evening of the assassination I went to my bed as usual, sensing nothing, foreseeing nothing, and at dawn next morning, hours before the messenger arrived to deliver the news, I was awakened by the noise of the chanting and of the heaving and crashing that accompanied it. For just one brief and heady moment I mistook the sounds for an outburst of popular joy and thought that the final step of our Project had been achieved to widespread acclaim, but then as the words became audible I felt the weight of the lioness upon me and was aware that all was over.

I went to the window, drew on my cloak and waited quietly for the guards to come and arrest me and deal with me as they had the statues: I did not like to be caught by such people in my bedwear. But after several groups of militants had passed by without so much as a glance at my door I knew that for some reason or other – age, significance, insignificance, or simply my knack of ridding a certain important lady of her headaches – I was to be spared. In the climate of ugly furore in which the city was now caught, the realization did little to brighten my mood.

'From him who was a foe of his fatherland let his honours be taken away; let the honours of the murderer be taken away; let the Monster be dragged in the dust. The foe of his fatherland, the murderer, the gladiator, in the charnel house let him be mangled. He is foe to the gods, slayer of the Senate, foe to the gods, murderer of the Senate, foe of the gods, foe of all mankind. Cast the gladiator into the charnel house. He who slew the Senate, let him be dragged with the hook; he who slew the guiltless, let him be dragged with the hook. He who spared not his own blood, he who plundered and slew and respected not the testaments of the dead, let him be dragged with the hook; let the Monster be dragged in the dust. The statues of the murderer and the gladiator, let them be cast down. Let his memory be utterly wiped away; let his name be erased from all records, public and private; let his effigies be effaced; let the very time be lost to us during which this scourge lay upon the State. Shame to him, shame everlasting. In the manner of our forefathers, let the body of the Monster be dug up and dragged by the hook, dragged by the hook until no trace remain.'

The chant is crass and repetitive but its burden is clear: scratch, wipe, rub, obliterate, Until No Trace Remain. And hard though it is to credit in these days of lax workmanship, by sundown of the very same day this exacting condition was almost completely fulfilled – at least as regards the cleansing of the actual capital; although thanks to the burning of the Archives much work in this direction had naturally been done already. The 'Monster's' body was in fact buried secretly and in great haste, so that when it came to the ceremonial dragging the organizers had to make do with a surrogate corpse affixed to the end of the hook in its stead, but as far as I could see this was the only makeshift element in the entire day's proceedings. Everything else was an expression of Roman efficiency at its bluntest and best.

LATE NIGHT TO DAWN (i.e. the precious lull before news of the assassination had spread): real enactment of the Edict of Condemnation, consisting in the bodily suppression of all closely implicated or connected persons and destruction of all compromising material.

DAWN TO NOON: Proclamation of the Edict in various points of the city and strategic incitement of the mob (hence the early morning noises heard by me) in order to make sure that all the heavier tasks such as statue toppling, erasure of marble and stone inscriptions and the like, were carried out by the crowd itself – zealously, immediately and free of any charge.

AFTERNOON TILL NIGHTFALL: For the undiscerning, continuation of the above; for a more select audience, of which I reluctantly decided it was wiser for me to form part; ceremonial enactment of the Edict and performance of relative rites of purification.

Roughly six-and-a-half years have now passed since the staging of this last event, and with the gradual rotting of their habitat many of my memories, especially the more recent ones, have a tendency to turn pale and flaccid like insects that live under stones. This particular one, however, which I would dearly like to see attenuated, remains obstinately vivid and fresh.

The ceremony took place, I recall, inside the precincts of the Imperial Palace; not in the main courtyard, but in the one adjacent to the barracks, which was larger and better drained. From the point of view of organization, as I have just said, it was an extremely impressive occasion – especially when you think of the haste with which everything must have been got together. Ample seating was provided, refreshments were available, and a written list of items, rather like an agenda or a theatre programme, could also be obtained on entry, although in the end of course there were not enough of these lists to go round, the attendance being enormous. As I heard someone seated close behind me remark admiringly, apart from the scale and unusual nature of the entertainment, it was like a very smart and successful supper party.

First on the list came the dispatch of the imperial pets and other so-termed 'domestic' animals. By which was meant evidently not the fowl or pigs or cattle but the hunting-dogs and saddle-horses and so forth – direct skin-to-skin contact being the criterion of elimination. A team of chariot horses was mentioned also which the 'Monster' had allegedly driven himself on more than one occasion and thus – or so ran the explanation on the programme – 'cannot be reasonably held to have escaped contagion by the accursed hand'; but when this item was reached it was announced that these particular horses had since been examined by the priests and found to be untainted (i.e. somebody important, perhaps one of the priests themselves, had taken a liking to them), and that only their harness need therefore be destroyed, and of it only their reins. (Well, say I, and wasn't that fortunate for the purchaser? Only the reins.)

In this opening part of the programme as throughout, the mode of operation was as follows: three separate teams of eight individuals worked simultaneously in triangle formation in the centre of the square, turning their hands indifferently to kniving, pounding or burning as required. These executive teams were aided, apart from numerous sweepers and cleaners, by twenty or so porters who unloaded the material to be eliminated – live or no as may be – on the one side, and then crossed rapidly to the other to remove the detritus – carcass or ashes depending – and load it on to another set of waiting vehicles, ducking as they did so, so as not to impede the spectators' vision.

I do not know about the others present, but I would have welcomed an impediment to mine. After the animals, in what I presumed was a calculatedly offensive sequence (but increasingly wonder nowadays if it necessarily is), came the retainers. Announced was a token group of a mere twenty people, four from each category: concubines, domestic staff, secretarial staff, advisory staff, and personal bodyguards. Actually brought in for disposal, however, was a much larger group totalling, I would say, closer to a hundred head.

I think it unlikely that any of these victims were known to me personally: as I said, the real object of the purge had already been achieved, and anyone truly close to the Emperor must therefore have been dead for hours. Nor am I squeamish; I have watched animals die (and humans too for that matter) purposely, often, and nearly always with complete detachment. Moreover, the craft of the executioners in this case was such that no victim suffered any more than was strictly necessary, for this was a ritual they were performing, not entertainment. Nevertheless, I assure you, not even for the sake of prudence could I bring myself to follow either of these stages of the proceedings or so much as pretend to do so, and from the first squeak of the first pet monkey, through all of the yelping and screeching and baying and neighing and crying that followed, down to the last faint protest of the young commander of the guard – very similar, this, I could not help noticing, to the opening noise made by the monkey – I sat with my head bent and watched instead the shapes and patterns of the pebbles on the ground. So it has come to this, I thought dully, too numbed to feel any distinct emotion. So much study, so much striving, such hopes, such dreams, and it has come to this.

On the heels of the appurtenances – and when I say heels I mean it literally because so smooth and quick was the fetching and carrying that the first case of scrolls almost touched the feet of the last victim lolling from the stretcher as it was dragged away – came the inanimate: viz., the coffers containing the private papers and correspondence, the clothes and jewellery and personal effects, the books (purposely very few of these, as you can imagine, in order to expose to the public their owner's disgraceful ignorance), the tableware, furnishings, carriage interiors, cushions, hangings and the other thousand-and-one articles of everyday use with which, inadvertently or not, the 'Monster's' body might have come into contact.

This less truculent type of destruction I found I could watch without much trouble and therefore did so, and diligently, because among so many craning heads my solitary bowed one was beginning to look a little conspicuous. Although here again when it came to certain very personal articles – the forked stick, for instance, which its owner had used for mushroom picking, or the special device which I had invented for him to help hide the lower deformity – I had occasionally to look down once more and transfer my attention to the pebbles.

Three hours passed in this way, if not more, during which time I behaved myself with all the command I could muster. I kept my head up as much as possible, I spoke once or twice to my neighbours, I may even have managed a smile. When it came to the last item on the agenda, however: the scouring and fumigation of the private apartments, an ancient and ugly rite which I knew envisaged several even more severe measures than those adopted so far, I felt I had had enough. And excusing myself vaguely on grounds of age and lameness to whoever happened to be listening, I backed away from the procession as it began to form and made my exit.

Passing through the gate on my way out I bumped into a fellow doctor, also leaving. Knowing him for a shrewd and intelligent man, if a shade slow in his thinking, I asked him quietly as we came away whether certain things about the performance we had just seen had not struck him as suspect: the speed, for instance, with which it had been carried out, the rigour of the executions? Romans were on the whole a thrifty and hard-headed lot, I reminded him; was it not unusual to say the least to see able-bodied slaves and fat glossy animals sent to the slaughter like that in the name of religious ideal, and not even a chance of eating the animals afterwards? Didn't he find such measures a trifle extreme?

My colleague appeared to chew on the question – inconvenienced by it as if it were fibrous. No, he said at length. No, he didn't think so really, not when one remembered the extremity of the evils they were intended to eradicate. 'Consider', he said, 'a rat, a louse, a bowel-worm. What do you do with such vermin? You stamp them into the ground, and then you fire the spot on which you have crushed them to make all clean again.' And he moved his gaze uneasily downward and kept it there, grinding his heel into the dust.

Without answering him, I turned away and left him to his grinding. Slowly, heavily for me, I picked my way through the rubble-laden streets and returned home to my study where I sat staring at the floor again until far into the night, trying to set order in my thoughts, trying to decide what must be done. Fame, Marcus Aurelius used to say, is worthless, and fame after death more worthless still, and my mood that night was such that I tended to agree with him. The Project was over, it had failed, and there was no more to be said. All the same, I could not help feeling that Marcus would not have been entirely happy to see the embodiment of all his hopes and dreams go down in history as a 'bowel-worm'. Even considering his austere contempt for public opinion, that, surely, I reasoned, was going a little too far?

The means I had at my disposal to remedy matters were few and frail, and they were growing frailer all the time. I had my brains, that is, my hands, and my memories. Before employing any of them, however, I decided that I must make just one attempt at finding out more about the actual circumstances of the murder. It was not that I needed any extra confirmation, you must understand, it was simply that this is the way I am made.

★

When I give this account of the Condemnation to Cassius, as I do almost immediately at the very start of our conversations, thinking to make a big impression on him and gain sympathy for my cause, his unencouraging comment is merely to hiccough and say that his own verdict coincides more or less with that of my medical colleague.

9

Only, he adds, being fussy in his speech he wouldn't perhaps have used the term 'bowel-worm' himself, but another, slightly more elegant.

He was not in Rome at the time himself, but the news reached him punctually as always and he is perfectly satisfied that no matter how quickly and drastically it may have been effected, the Condemnation was a wise and necessary measure of purification and no more than that. He doubts too that it even was quite as drastic as I would have him believe: he cannot vouch for the livestock but certainly a fair amount of furniture and stuff belonging to the Emperor went up to auction later because he knows people who bought pieces, and at very good prices too. How they could have done so he does not know, but that is the way people are. Anything for a bargain. He has no love for our present ruler and no particular desire to defend him; he is merely sure that my accusation of a cover-up is inexact.

Likewise, he says, he is equally well satisfied that the burning of the Archives, on which I put so sinister an interpretation, was a straightforward accident, although he can well understand my dismay at losing my writings and my desire to find a culprit to put the blame on – as a fellow writer no doubt he would feel that way himself in my position. Again, he was absent when the event took place, but he chanced to meet the Head Librarian at a reception not long afterwards and was assured by him personally that the fire was caused by the upsetting of an oil-lamp and an unfortunate change in the wind just as the first outbreak of flames was being brought safely under control. The reason why it was the recent records to go and not the others was very simple according to the Head Librarian: the hide they were written on was newer and fattier and therefore burned faster, and that was all there was to it. It is easy, Cassius winds up with another hiccough, to point to a pile of ashes and say, Look, I have corroboration for what I allege because all the documents have indeed been destroyed and all the witnesses are indeed dead and this is all there is left. But this – corroboration through lack of corroboration – is a paradox, and paradoxes are empty things that get you nowhere, and some people say they are evil as well – and he, Cassius, tends to agree with them. So far he has promised me nothing but his ears, but he is afraid I will not have even those for long unless I am able to back up my case with something a little more substantial than a paradox.

My need for the Senator's ears being what it is, I naturally do my best to oblige with all I can offer in the way of substance. Although thanks to the violence of the Purge it is not much.

DE MINIMIS NON CURAT PRÆTOR
(The Praetor has no time for little things or little people.)

My old and at one time close professional acquaintance, the Imperial Washer-in-Chief-and-Superintendent-Layer-Out-of-Corpses, was as short as his title was long. In his laboratory, which had been fitted out to his own specifications, stools and benches were at knee-level and the work-slabs not much higher – a touch which lent a rather homely feel to what would otherwise have been a dank and miserable place.

I entered the room gingerly – it was quite some years now since I had set foot there but I had not forgotten in the meantime how treacherous the floor was – and looked about me. Keeping my hat well down over my eyes and my scarf across my mouth, for I was anxious for my visit to remain as private as possible.

The idea of consulting this particular source for the information I needed had come to me, as I said, only after a certain delay. I had realized immediately, even as I sat there in the smoke-ridden square on the day of the Condemnation watching the elimination-squads go about their business, that the clearance would never be complete; that in the end, no matter how hard the squads worked, there was bound to be some minor witness somewhere or some tiny scrap of evidence that would escape their notice. It only stood to reason; it was like de-nitting a head: when you have a great mass of hair and a great number of insects it is almost a postulate of logic that however careful you are there is always the odd nit that slips through the comb. Not until a week or so had passed, though, and I had nearly bored a hole in the floor of my study by all my staring, had it occurred to me just who the escaped nit would most likely be. And this too was a matter of logic: I had not thought of the Chief Body-Washer because no one thought of him, ever. And it was because nobody ever thought of him, or paid any attention to him whatever beyond the delivering of dirty corpses to one door of his laboratory and the collecting of clean ones at the other, that he was still alive and in possession, or so I hoped, of the information I required.

The Chief Body-Washer was in fact very much alive, but I had to draw quite near to him to make sure of this, since he was taking what was evidently a much-needed rest from his duties – exceptionally heavy of late – and had chosen to do so stretched out on one of the slabs in the company of his charges.

There he lay on his improvised bed, looking rosy and comfortable and younger than I had ever seen him, his head propped by a cushion, his feet by another; asleep, but only the way a dog is. He opened an eye as soon as I approached the slab, recognizing me at once, despite the hat and scarf, despite the intervening years.

'Well,' he said. 'So. The great Galen,' but with no surprise in his voice whatever, much as if saying 'the next month' or 'the left shoe'. 'The great Galen of Pergamos in person in my humble workshop. Times are changing indeed. Another few weeks and, who knows? I may be privileged to receive a visit from our Prince himself.'

I bent down critically to scan the Washer's face for traces of rancour at my coming here without warning to presume on his services yet again – I have no patience with rancour, I ride over it like a bull over lettuce – but thankfully there were none. So I smiled and helped the little man to rise. Noticing as I did so how much suppler he was than myself; not only rosier and younger-looking, but much, much suppler. Did smallness make for longevity, I wondered briefly? But then I thought of butterflies and elephants and decided that it did not.

It had been my intention to move slowly with my friend the Body-Washer, explaining to him first the circumstances of my visit and why I had not made it earlier (avoiding, naturally, all references to nits), but the mention of the Prince seemed to me to provide an opening that was too handy to be missed.

'Then he could do no worse,' I put in quickly. 'The Prince, I mean, our new Prince. If, like myself, he is a curious man and fond of knowledge, there are many worse places he could choose to visit than this, wouldn't you agree? Our politicians seem to believe – and to act on the belief – that dead men cannot speak, but you know that is not the way I see it. No, my view has always been the reverse: that dead men speak very clearly – to those who know how to listen.'

The move may have been too quick, however, and too glib. The undertaker's lips folded into a pleat which could have meant anything or nothing at all, and he made no sign of having heard me other than to seat himself on one of his toy stools and indicate to me to do the same.

It being too late to go back now, I thought I might as well go forward. 'Besides,' I went on, lowering my voice significantly as I lowered my body: the room was large and rang like a cave, 'I have a feeling that you *did* receive a visit of the kind only recently. Reflect carefully: I am referring not to our present ruler but to his predecessor. And I am referring not to a visit of courtesy on the Emperor's part either, still less one of those fleeting visits he used to pay you in the past on his way to you-know-where, but a different kind of visit altogether. A, should we say, uniquely professional visit which we would all of us prefer he had never paid. Did something of the sort not take place, or am I mistaken?'

The pleat, without moving, contrived to display a certain cross-ness. Or perhaps it was dismay. I shifted uncomfortably on my stool. I do not hold with sitting at the best of times: it is an unnatural position and ruinous to the digestion. But here I was not even sitting, I was crouching; I was bending double. However, as over the matter of the nits, delicacy prompted me to silence.

'It is quite safe for you to speak,' I urged. 'I trust your discretion entirely or I would not be squatting,' I corrected myself, 'sitting here before you dressed in this unusual attire,' and I indicated the head-covering, 'when a word from you to the authorities would put me in deepest trouble – and you can trust mine. What you tell me will go no further. It never has done in the past, and it will not do so now. I assure you,' and on my lips I made the sign which we had so often used to communicate with one another in the old days, hoping that it would awaken memories, 'my mouth is full of wine.'

The sign worked. The midget's face relaxed and he made an identical sign back at me, accompanied by a gargling noise. 'So is mine,' he said, 'so is mine.' Then for the first time he smiled. 'Ah, Galen, Galen,' he said (he had the edge over me here, for hard as I tried I just could not remember his name, and asking was out of the question), 'inquisitive as ever, I am glad to see, but when will you learn that there are some things better left *un*probed? What makes you think the Emperor's body was lodged here, I would like to know?

What makes you think it was lodged anywhere? Doesn't news reach you? Didn't you hear how things went? Don't you know who the murderers were, and how desperate their action? And don't you know that their thirst for revenge against their cruel master was so great that they denied him burial and popped him into a sack instead and threw him into the river so that he would be carried out to sea and washed forever back and forth by the tides, and find no peace, and his soul never rest? Don't you know all these things? Of course you do. So what makes you think, if it was thrown into a sack like a pile of rubbish, that the body sojourned here? Rubbish is not laundered, surely, before it is thrown away?'

The Chief Body-Washer had a point here, of course, but to understand fully what he was alluding to, we must consider the official account of the assassination in detail. It was as follows: that the Emperor, dissatisfied with his domestic staff as he was with everything else, had planned a decimation of all his retainers, concubines included, on quasi-military lines. A secret list was allegedly drawn up by him of the names of those he most wanted to be rid of, and then left lying about in his boudoir where it was discovered by chance by a page. The page read this list, grasped its import immediately (in this I had already detected a weakness: since when do pages grasp anything immediately?), and took it hot-foot to show to Marcia, the Emperor's notorious Chief Concubine, whose name headed the list. This resolute female, so the story went, quite at her ease in matters of vice and intrigue, lost no time but served poisoned soup to her lover that very evening as he lay in his bath – whistling, no doubt, as was his regrettable habit. In her haste, however, Marcia overdid the dose, and the Emperor, instead of succumbing to the poison, vomited it all up again. After which he turned very sour and intractable, as can be imagined, and panic ensued. All would have been lost – it was said factions were already beginning to form amongst the slaves, some in favour of continuing the rebellion, some for quashing it, some for abandoning it altogether and running for their lives – had not Marcia again taken a strong hand: or, rather, *hired* a strong hand, in the person of a professional wrestler with a hitherto unbeaten record and a pair of arms on him like pigs' haunches. This man, in exchange for a certain quantity of the Concubine's jewels – fistful, bagful, bucketful; versions differed a little as to the exact price – was introduced with all possible speed into the Emperor's chambers through a window,

15

where he neatly performed the necessary deed by the simple means of a lute-string drawn tight around the Emperor's throat and held there for some minutes. (Simple? With a man the Emperor's size and strength? Well, let us say simple in the telling.)

This, then, was the story, but I could see from the curl in his mouth as he spoke the word 'rubbish' that the Chief Body-Washer believed just about as much of it as I did: that is to say, not a word.

'So,' I said, returning to his question and giving what I thought was a very compact answer, 'true, rubbish is not laundered. But it sometimes strikes me that it should be when so much of it is put about, and so much of it is believed, and so much of it is so very, very foul.'

The midget's eyebrows – or the skin where the eyebrows should have been – rose and he extended his elegant little fingers and set them together like crossbeams. It looked as if he was beginning to enjoy the conversation. 'Your brain moves fast, Galen,' he said, 'it always did. But mine does not, I am afraid, and you must have patience with me. It is a very curious thing you say there. I wonder what you mean by it? That the slaves were not responsible for the murder? Or that they were, but gave their master a proper burial none the less? Or that someone else did? Or what?'

I envy people who can confess like that to slowness of understanding. I never can myself, and this sometimes gets me into trouble. 'I mean,' I said carefully, 'simply this: that while I think it was definitely in the interest of the murderers – *whoever* they may have been: slaves, freedmen, senators, soldiers, shopkeepers or even a company of travelling fruit-pickers – to cause the Emperor's body to disappear as soon as possible, I do not think they were quite so pitiless or impious as to waive the rites of burial entirely. It is a feeling I have,' I went on, 'nothing more. I have noticed that people – and animals too for that matter – after a violent deed will hesitate to commit another and will generally opt to do something gentle instead – like lick their paws, or weep, or sing, or go to sleep. I think the Emperor was slain brutally enough, but I think he was given a respectful if hurried funeral afterwards. And I think that *you*,' and I drew myself up tall on the stool and laid an accusing finger on my listener's breastbone: not for nothing am I the terror of generations of students, '*you* prepared him for it.'

My hunch was correct, as I had known all along it would be. The Chief Body-Washer dismantled the crossbeams and spread them wide in sign of submission. Very well, he admitted, and if this were so? He was not saying that it was, mind you, but if it *were* – then what was it exactly that I would like to know?

Why, everything, I told him quickly before he had time to reflect and reimpose the conditional. I wanted to know everything. Every single detail he could remember. I wanted to know how the body was clothed, and what state the clothes were in, and what marks they bore, and what marks the body bore. And not only the wounds: I wanted to know how long the hair was, how long the nails, how clean the teeth, how many flea-bites had been counted on the skin and how many freckles. And I also wanted to know whether, besides being washed, the Emperor's body had also been prepared for embalmment, and if so, what had been found on the *in*side as well as the out.

The undertaker sighed and looked at me penetratingly. 'You *want* to know?' he asked. 'You are sure it is something you truly *want*?'

From the way he spoke I realized that my friend the Washer understood a great deal more than I gave him credit for. I corrected myself. 'I need to know,' I replied, 'if the distinction is of any importance. Why do you ask? Was the end so very bad, then?'

The little man spread his hands again and shrugged. 'Perhaps,' he said; 'perhaps not. You will have to decide yourself. I see so many ends, I am afraid I have lost the power to judge.'

But not, fortunately, or so it would seem from the description the Washer now gave me and which I reproduce here in abbreviated form, cutting out all his asides and comments and most of his surmises, not the power to observe.

CLOTHING: None. The body was delivered wrapped in a woollen blanket, but otherwise naked. It bore strap-marks, however, and buckle-marks and signs of chafing. Indicating that when the Emperor met his death he was dressed in full fighting gear and had been for some time? Yes, indicating I think just this.

HAIR: Recently cut, very recently washed, recently dressed, but tousled and damp with sweat. Perfumed. Thin over dome of head, profuse and curly at sides and nape. Faint traces of gold-dust on scalp.

HEAD: Skull unmarked; beard trim, unsoiled, ungilded; eyelids and mouth open but still malleable. Teeth clean and sound, central-left incisor badly chipped; tongue slightly swollen on left-hand side as if from biting; no sign of bleeding, no food-remains in oral cavity. Facial expression contorted (which both the Washer and myself agreed, meant very little).

NECK: Pliable, unmarked save for a light ring of grime lodged in the skin-folds of the throat.

FEET AND RIGHT HAND: Sweaty, grimy, bloodstained. No wounds, no blemishes. Well cared for. Very large.

LEFT HAND: Missing.

LEGS AND ARMS: Smooth, muscular, depilated, hairs showing signs of regrowth. Heavily bloodstained. Left arm much more developed than right. Traces of numerous scratches and gashes on all four limbs, and of two severe wounds on left thigh and forearm, all of them healed. Ubiquitous strap-marks.

LOWER TORSO: Back and buttocks normal, well formed, unharmed. Abdomen and genitals not depilated, heavily blood-drenched, the latter integral. Deep but neat incision, roughly the size of a child's footprint, in right groin. Probably (but, said the Chief Body-Washer, the corpse being so fresh it was hard to tell) inflicted after death, and probably (say I) performed with good intentions: the murderers, i.e. as with the removal of the hand, were concerned merely to ameliorate the body before burial.

UPPER TORSO: Broad, well muscled, depilated to waist-level. Shoulders bore signs of armour-straps. Back presented moles, scars and scratches, but otherwise no abnormalities. Chest lacerated by a dozen or more wounds grouped together in the region of the heart, caused by a sharp-bladed instrument or instruments, presumably knife or dagger. Ribcage shattered, lungs and heart severely damaged; death to be imputed to this latter.

And this was all that my friend the Chief Body-Washer had to tell me. Preparation for embalmment was not carried out, nor was any particular service requested of him other than the routine procedure of cleansing and composing the corpse. As soon as this was completed, the jaw had been tied, the eyelids made fast with resin, and the Emperor rolled up in his blanket once again and left in the ante-chamber, ready for consignment to those who had brought him.

As to who these bearers were, the undertaker said he could say nothing as he had been careful not to find out, hiding himself prudently in a tub of dirty rags until they had taken their burden and departed. Before I left he showed me how he had accomplished this. I was fascinated; he fitted into the tub in an almost magical way, limp and folded, just like a bundle of linen. I have never seen anything so neat and compact in my life, although perhaps more extraordinary still was seeing him come out again.

As I took my leave, I asked the little undertaker whether he was still frightened of a belated visit from the assassins, but he said no, not any longer, he reckoned that danger was past now. And what if my precautions for secrecy were insufficient and our present conversation became known, I enquired?

The silky forehead crinkled briefly and then cleared again. In that case, he said, he thought it would be me, not himself, who would have to repair to a suitable hiding-place. And he bowed low and bade me take my turn at entering the tub.

I bowed back to decline the offer, turned, and walked towards the door. 'And the other body?' I asked as if in afterthought as I crossed the threshold, half-hoping that the question would not be heard. 'Hers, I mean.'

'In the best of health, obviously,' the Washer's voice reached me, 'seeing that we are told she is married off already to some high-placed slave and is about to receive a large State pension in reward for her pains.'

The tone was flat, ironic, and I felt a spasm, as if a frog had entered my stomach and made a large jump inside. 'You saw it also then?' I asked. 'It too was entrusted to your care?'

'I saw it also,' the voice confirmed. 'But this time it is I who will decide what you need to know and what you don't. And more than that, believe me, Galen, you do not need to know. I saw the body, and you can take it from me that she too is dead.'

★

When I tell him this second story of mine, Cassius's response is if anything less encouraging still. Although not a paradox, it is clear that the argument is just as foreign to him and just as distasteful. He is well aware, he says, that I have always adopted unconventional methods in my own profession, and am famous for barging into the sickroom and tearing up my patients' astral charts and pummelling their stomachs instead and sniffing their urine and goodness knows what other weirdities. But such an approach, while it may work reasonably well in medicine, is shockingly out of place when it comes to the writing of history. Medicine too, to some extent (which is no doubt why I have made myself so many enemies among my colleagues), but history is indissolubly linked with the concept of Authority: it is made by those in Authority, it is about those in Authority, it is recorded by those in Authority (or when it isn't, should be), always in a suitably dignified and authoritative manner, and it very properly takes the pronouncements of Authority as its sole touchstone for the truth. What I am now asking, on the other hand, is that he, Cassius, Senator and son of a senator, lay aside the well-tried and reliable touchstone – not only, but that he actually allow its reliability to be placed in question – on the basis of rival pronouncements issuing from such lofty founts, if you please, as the mouth of a midget undertaker and the scars of a mutilated corpse. Do I take him for a subversive, or a traitor to his calling, or what do I take him for?

To this I have a ready answer, and quietly, but with a tone in my voice that would wrest shame from the backside of a rhino, I say that before all else I take His Excellency for an upright and gracious man who would never dismiss a supplicant without granting him a fair hearing. (This, incidentally, was a tip I learnt from Marcus Aurelius: Let a man know what a high opinion you have of him, and there is a chance that he may live up to it.)

The tip seems to work. Ah, yes, well, says Cassius. Um. Ah. Yes. A fair hearing, of course, of course, and then changes the slant of the conversation. 'Incidentally,' he asks, 'what happened to the midget in the end? You did not say.'

It is my turn now to feel a slight twinge of shame. 'I am afraid I do not know, Excellency,' I admit, 'for the very simple reason that the moment I left the little man's workshop I straight away went and forgot all about him again. With such a flair for obscurity, though, I comfort myself that he was unmolested and is still plying his trade tranquilly to this day. If Your Excellency likes I could make enquiries.'

20

His Excellency does not like. I can see only his shadow but have the impression that he jabs his fingers in the air like snails' horns: undertakers, like paradoxes, are reputed to bring bad luck. No, no, no, he says hurriedly, no need for that, no need for that, my stories are quite taxing enough in themselves. First the knacker's yard, then the morgue; he dreads to think where they will lead us next.

★

So, as I said, not at all a promising beginning that I make here with the Senator, but I suppose I must be grateful that there is to be a next. Belief or unbelief on his part, it seems I am at least to be allowed to go on talking.

VERBA VOLANT, SCRIPTA MANENT

(But it goes without saying that writings do not
remain if they are burnt, and burnt again.)

The period that followed the events I have just described was a time
of acute political and social turmoil. Not only I, but everyone I
spoke to, everyone I met, even my barber and the tradesmen who
came to deliver their wares, crept about the place like the survivors of
an earthquake: dazed, uncomprehending; hands, so to speak, crossed
over their heads as if fearful of other bits of masonry still to fall. As
happens after an earthquake, however, the dust finally settled on
the ruins and, when it did, the new conformation of the landscape
emerged in all its clarity. It took a little time, of course, these things
do. Thus, over the next five months or so we had two interim rulers,
sent like slaves to the lavatory to keep the seat warm for their master
who follows; we had a couple more assassinations as these temporary
occupants were shifted aside; and mingled with all this we had rioting
and looting and uproar, and the post of Head of State being put
up to public auction as if it were a sheep or a sack of lentils. But
before half a year had expired (which, when you think of his impatience in most things, is a decent enough interval) the man behind
the whole operation, none other than our present ruler, Septimius
Severus that is, had put an end to all this foolery and come into his
own.

Strengthened in my resolve by my brief visit to the Washer,
strengthened in particular by the description he gave me which, more
than any commitment to an abstraction be it ever so lofty, has been
responsible for kindling my anger and keeping it alight throughout.
I spent the period myself in the only useful way I knew how: I shut
myself in my study in the sole company of my trusted old secretary
Philostratus and together we began to write. Everything, for a second
time, from beginning to end. The text being now familiar to us, it
took us just under the six months to complete, although I confess we

22

cut a few corners here and there this time around and slid over the philosophical parts – long in the burnt original – quickly and lightly, like children over a marble floor. On the very same evening I had finished dictation, however – punctually, relentlessly and without any appreciable change in method – my study was broken into, the manuscript in question, together with several other notes and letters, reduced once more to ashes, and the ashes crammed into the mouth of my beloved amanuensis who died three days later from the shock and the maltreatment he had received.

The message, although unwritten and unsigned, took little deciphering: I was not going to be allowed to spoil things for our new Emperor Severus, not going to be allowed to scatter inconvenient crumbs over his nice clean-swept floor. His regard for me – or perhaps his wife's regard for me, for Severus himself does not suffer from headaches or anything else and consequently has never had much time for doctors – was still sufficient to prevent him from striking my actual person, but if I wanted to avoid any further unpleasantness on the lines of this present one, I was to keep my knowledge to myself for the few years that remained for me to live and then take it with me obligingly to the grave.

Realizing that the informer was, could only be, a member of my own household and quite an intimate one at that, I sent back to Severus a suitably clear answer via the same channel. I waited until the day after Philostratus's death; then, having washed his poor offended old body myself and prepared it for burial (effecting while I was about it a quick probe into the stomach to see if the ashes had filtered down that far and if so to what effect, for it is an inflexible rule of my school that personal feelings never be allowed to interfere with science), I summoned up my entire staff and announced to them solemnly that I was putting an end to my literary career.

The decision, I said, was not only a prudential one, taken in their interests and my own, but also aesthetic: I had seen so many corpses and ashes of late that I could take no more of them. I sent for my writing materials – it was the crass language that I knew Severus would appreciate – and pens, styli, inks and scrolls and tablets, I cast them in a heap on to the carriage where the body of my secretary was already laid. I did not think that Philostratus would mind; in its way it seemed a very fitting send-off for a scribe. 'There,' I said. 'You are all of you my witnesses. The man who lies here before us acted in life as my right hand, and now that he is dead it is as if my right hand had been cut from my body. I swear by all that is sacred to me' (in fact very little, but this it was not given to any of my subordinates save Philostratus himself to know) 'that I will write no more.'

And no more I did. Fortunately, though, as far as my present and last attempt at recording is concerned, I said nothing about talking.

If my listener shows no discouraging reaction to this third short and rather sad story, it is because I am careful not to tell it to him. I can see there will be difficulties enough to contend with in obtaining Cassius's help without my going and compounding them with fright. True, six years is a long stretch of time, and true, during this time Severus has risen and risen and I have sunk and sunk so that the distance that divides us is now very great indeed, and I very much doubt in consequence that my movements of today – infirm and rheumaticky as they have become – are of much interest to his busy imperial ear. The doctor is seeing a new patient, is he? is what he probably thinks – when and if he is informed of the fact. Let him do so then, and good luck to the patient; I wouldn't let the old fumbler anywhere near me myself. This, I think, is the extent of the imperial concern in my activities. But still, Cassius is no lion exactly, and I do not deem it either politic or necessary to inform him of the fate of my previous literary collaborator. Or even very tactful. As I say, I foresee trouble enough with him as it is. When he asks me, therefore, as he does punctually and a little nervously at this point, why it is that I do not act as my own author when I have written so copiously in the past and so well, I merely point to the ugly webs that now curtain my eyes almost completely and say, 'Because, alas, Excellency, factors over which I have no control intervene and prevent me from doing so.' It is, after all, the truth, so far as it goes.

PART II

THE ACCUSATIONS

SINE IRA ET STUDIO

(How history should be written, according to Tacitus: impartially, without bias.)

Six years. Yes, it is six years now since Severus's grisly warning was delivered, and in these six years it has never once seriously crossed my mind that I could do anything but heed it. I have wanted to disregard it, longed to disregard it. I have thought up fanciful stratagems – like committing my memories to slabs of stone and burying them underground, like sewing them into a winding-sheet and then doing the same, like devising an invisible ink or a secret code in which to write them, or even teaching them to one of these wondrous talking birds that I am told can be purchased in foreign markets, although at an exorbitant price; but I have never, or not until very recently, that is, thought that a real, practicable way existed of eluding the veto. The official ban on writing about the period has been lifted – this was done some months ago now, when the Edict of Condemnation was repealed – but I know that the lifting does not apply to me.

However, life, as my nurse used to say when preparing her philtres at forty-seven for yet another fugitive suitor, is full of surprises; you never know what it has in store for you. And now, just as I am preparing to conform to the final clause of Severus's missive – for I am fast approaching seventy and am grown frail and nearly blind and know from long experience of others that the end cannot be far – life springs one of its surprises on me and sends me Cassius. Or, rather, sends Cassius me. The summons itself comes as a surprise. My practice, as can only be expected, has dwindled away almost to nothing. Severus's wife has found other ways of dealing with her migraines and has long since withdrawn her patronage. Likewise the rest of the fashionable world. I still have a few regular patients whom I visit from time to time – most of them as old as myself and as doddery, who dislike change and put up with my slowness on this account, but even they tend to turn to my assistants when they are really ill, and a new patient, and a youngish one at that, has not come my way for a long, long time. However, perhaps because he is of provincial stock and does not move with the times, perhaps because he has spent so much time away from the capital that he has lost his contacts, or perhaps simply because he has consulted all the other practitioners already and I am the only one there is left, the Senator and writer Cassius Dio Coccceianus, on one of his rare visits to Rome and at the onset of one of his not-so-rare bouts of prickly feet, sends for me, and I am quick – well, quick as I can be – to obey the summons.

I do not recognize immediately, mind you, that in the person of the lively and bumptious little statesman with his horror of disease, Fate is offering me a loophole – a possible vehicle on which to load my thoughts and see them trundle off more or less comfortably towards posterity. But then the Senator takes a little getting to know, and I am not, as I said, looking for loopholes any more or hoping to find any.

When the idea of using him as such begins to dawn on me though, as it does about half-way through the visit when behind the bluster and gossip and chatter I perceive signs of a frank and inquisitive mind and a generosity to match it, it dawns bright and almost rosy. I run through the advantages in my head. First, I tell myself, Cassius at thirty-five is already a writer of some repute which, although it may not mean he is a good writer, means that his works will have a better chance of survival than most. Second, Cassius *himself* looks to me, even after so short an examination, to have a better chance of survival than most, and his cautious nature can only enhance it. Third, his reputation for hypochondria ensures that my visits will not arouse suspicion in the wrong quarters – or not for quite some while. And last and best of all, he tells me he is already engaged in writing about the very period I am concerned with and, when I put forward, very tentatively, my request, professes himself willing to talk about it and – more important still – to listen.

Why not? he says cheerfully, meaning, I think, no discourtesy. The physician's viewpoint is an unusual one for sure, but interesting. I must, in a manner of speaking, have been close to my imperial patrons during the years I served them. My position, of course, would have been rather *too* close for correct observation, rather like that, shall we say, of a flea to its host. And like a flea of its host, all I will have been able to catch sight of is patches of skin – skin and boils and rashes and humours (a laugh here, but not an unkind one); but all the same, he, Cassius, is the last person to underrate the importance of humours when it comes to understanding a person and, all things considered, he would be very happy to listen to what I have to say.

So, still very tentatively, I begin my stories, sounding out as I go the trustworthiness of this unlikely and unlooked-for vehicle, and trying to discover how best it is to be driven.

The reception of the stories, as we have already seen, is not very promising, nor is the testing of the vehicle. At the first hump it wobbles, slides, sticks in the mud; at the second, it threatens almost to turn over. On my next visit to the Senator's household, therefore, I try a different approach and, mindful of another saying of Marcus's, viz., that if you want a man to do what you tell him you must hear him out carefully first so that you can chart the territory of his mind, I offer no more stories but say diffidently instead that this time I would greatly appreciate it if it were Cassius himself who were to do the telling.

'When you spoke to me about your coming History,' I say, 'Your Excellency told me, if I remember rightly, that it is to be based, amongst other things, on your personal, live recollections of the Emperor Commodus. Perhaps you would be good enough to tell me what these recollections are, and – if it is not too much trouble – to give them to me in detail. All or some, as you see fit.'

Cassius is provincial, but of high enough rank for this not to bother him. Plus which he is a willing talker. He admits frankly that he has spent so much of his life away from the capital that his real face-to-face encounters with Commodus were in fact only two. ('And two,' he adds hurriedly, 'was more than enough.') He saw him, that is, at the beginning of the reign when, aged sixteen or thereabouts, he was taken by his father to the Senate to hear the young Emperor's inaugural speech to the assembly there, and he saw him towards the end of the reign, nearly twelve years later, in one of his astonishing exhibitions in the arena. This second occasion is naturally the one he remembers best and which made the greater impression. 'And naturally,' I concur politely, 'the one I would like to hear.'

Before he begins, however, Cassius goes on quickly, he has a question to put to me. Did he hear me aright about the medical assistance being free of charge? Is that indeed to be my part of the bargain? Because if so – and he takes hold of my hands and places them firmly on the back of his neck – then it is not only the feet, but he has a tiresome ache just about here which might benefit from my attention. Perhaps I could perform a spot of massage on it as he speaks?

I bow and comply. Nothing, I assure him, would give me greater pleasure. And it is not far from the truth: at least I can be said to have got a hold on my audience now. The description, however, which for the sake of accuracy I give here in more or less the Senator's own words, pleases me somewhat less.

'The month was August – although we were not then allowed to call it August, if you remember, one of our beloved Emperor's little vanities being to rename the months and almost everything else he could think of after himself. But the month was August. The day was hot and grey and clammy, with a faint wind from the south, hot and clammy too. A bad day for insects; a worse day for men.

'The Emperor had long since waived the custom of receiving personal greetings from members of the Senate before the opening of the games (one of the very few welcome innovations he ever made), so I was free to enter the amphitheatre directly. Which I did. I may tell you, Galen, that despite all the fuss and talk that had gone on beforehand I was not at all impressed by what I saw. The place was dusty and stifling. The awnings, true to rumour, had indeed been substituted by coloured ones, but they were of a brick-coloured shade and the light they shed on everyone and everything was livid and troublesome. It felt to me as if I had been introduced into the belly of a great beast which had had meat and vegetables for its dinner and hadn't bothered to chew them properly. We spectators being the meat, the decorations being the vegetables, if you catch my meaning.

'Although considerable headway at digestion, I will admit, had been made with the vegetables. The woodland effect which everyone had spoken about for weeks with bated breath as a delight and a bewitchment had, in fact, been created by the simple expedient of sawing off the branches of a few mangy trees, stuffing them into pots, and then grouping the pots in small clusters around the edges of the arena. It may conceivably have looked all right at the moment of planting, but by the time the spectators arrived, half the leaves were off the branches and the rest were badly wilting. We had been promised fountains and blossoms and perfume, but as I recall, no attempt at irrigation had been made other than the normal sluices; there were no flowers – August is a bad month for flowers, anyway, as any gardener will tell you – and the pervading smell was just what one expects to find in a covered enclosure containing hundreds of frightened animals and thousands of frightened people. Yes, frightened, we were frightened. I was frightened out of my wits and do not mind admitting it, and I think everyone else was frightened too. The Emperor's own safety, of course, had been amply guaranteed. The arena had been partitioned into four separate enclosures – allegedly for scenic reasons, but in reality to give the animals less chance of escape and less chance of inflicting harm. Around each partition a tall fence had been erected – double, with a kind of plank or passageway inbetween forming a gallery from which our brave Hercules of a hunter could hurl his weapons in safety and be refurnished with them by his assistants as he went along. A similar gallery ran also round the entire circumference of the arena, surmounted on the spectators' side by a net – full of holes and very flimsy. In addition to this, many of the smaller animals and nearly all of the birds had been tethered; the larger beasts were mostly hobbled as well; and the hippopotamus (there was only one of these creatures to the promised dozen), judging by the look of it, had been made groggy with drink. Thus the Emperor, you understand, had little to fear.

'For the onlookers, however, particularly for those seated like myself and my fellow senators close to the scene of action, things were very different. The Emperor was, true, a nifty marksman, but he was shooting fast and sometimes – if, for example, a bird took flight or a prey broke from its tether and made for the barriers – outwards. Thus, as the holes in the net testified, there was always the very real possibility of being hit by a stray shaft; just as there was also the very real possibility, if one had incurred the imperial displeasure in some way, which it was not hard to do, of being hit by a shaft that was not stray at all but purposely directed against one. It did not make for pleasant entertainment, I assure you.

'Another instance of his malice: the Emperor kept us waiting in the blistering purple heat of the amphitheatre for nearly a full hour before he made his appearance. I had a flask of water with me, which I alternatively drank from and sprinkled over my head, or I think

I would have passed out. The noise of the penned animals, some battened out of sight in cages, but most of them already on the floor, was atrocious. So, as I have already mentioned, was the stench: I can remember that my head ached for days afterwards.

'When the Emperor finally appeared, a great roar went up from the crowd (more of impatience, I judged, than enthusiasm) which swamped the playing of the musicians and robbed the ceremony of what little grace it might have had.

'He was dressed in his usual extravagant manner – white and gold drapery, more jewellery than a woman, and with the habitual nimbus of gold-dust powdering his hair. After strutting around a while so that everybody could admire his magnificence he then proceeded to undress in an equally extravagant manner until stripped to a lion-skin (dusted in gold, this too, but rather bedraggled when you saw it closely) which fell crosswise from his shoulder to just below the pelvis, and exposed his thighs and part of the buttocks. In profile, or when under stress, even the bulge of his unsightly deformity was visible.

'Oooh! Aaah! went the crowd, and he bowed to it as would a common gladiator. I have never seen anything sadder, but at the same time funnier or more ludicrous. O Magnificent One! O Tiger-slayer! O Hercules reborn! The irony of which a Roman crowd is capable when it says one thing with its words but quite another with its tone, has to be heard to be believed.

'Presiding over the hunt in quality of patroness was the Emperor's brash and shameless Chief Concubine Marcia – the one eventually responsible for the assassination. I remember her extremely clearly. A dreadful great bold-eyed, swaggering she-bear of a woman, clothed like her lover, or should I say *un*clothed like her lover, in a skimpy piece of animal hide, which covered the legs but left shoulders and one breast totally bare. My gaze was drawn to the last particular continuously. The nipple, I recall, was – concealed is not the right word, the effect was more one of emphasis, so let us say garnished – by a small golden cap which bobbed up and down with every movement of the breast without ever coming unloosed. I kept expecting it to fall; I could hardly take my eyes from it, but it never did, not even when the wearer jumped to her feet to cheer. Women are resourceful over their toilets of course, but to me this fact of the nipple-cap defied explanation and still does. Resin, could it have been? Honey? Or could the cap itself have been made in the shape of one of the suckers on an octopus's leg? I shall never know.'

I interrupt the Senator's account here for a moment, (a) to bring him back on his tracks again, and (b) to insinuate rather craftily that from one so bedazzled by a detail, inaccuracies about the rest of the proceedings are only to be expected. I do not tell him, however, that the substance used for Marcia's breast cover was in fact bone glue and gave off a horrible smell at close quarters, as this would merely be unkind.

Piqued, Cassius replies that what I say is nonsense, that he saw and followed everything, and far better than I could have done because his seat was that much nearer, and he is anyway far more knowledgeable about venery. He continues:

'And speaking of venery, the Emperor's performance by technical standards was good but not exceptional: his helpers did a lot of finishing-off of targets on the sly, the weapon-count was rigged and the true ratio between throws and hits was probably far lower than that announced. By political and human standards on the other hand, the performance was little short of disastrous. The ruler of the Roman State is, or should be, the most exalted and dignified being in the world. We know, alas, that this is not always so, and recently people have come to expect less and less of their Prince. However, to see the man who occupies this position cavorting round the public arena like a paid performer, leaping and grinning and shouting and bandying words with the onlookers, and waving to his concubine, and goodness knows what other fooleries besides – well, it was quite simply intolerable.

'And in fact it was not tolerated. The comment of the public, muted by fear but none the less unmistakable, was a sustained buzz of derision throughout. The Emperor, naturally, pretended not to notice, but towards the end, when the buzz turned to a howl and the gestures became more and more explicit and more and more abusive, he began to lose his temper. He had just killed an ostrich, I remember – a fine throw which hit the bird in full run and severed the neck from the body so cleanly that the poor beast continued to scamper headless for quite some number of paces before it fell to the ground. This was greeted by mirth, some faint cheering, and then, on top of the cheering, one of those incomparable noises (you know the sound I mean, half-way between a horse breaking wind and the rending of a sailcloth) for which the Roman mob is so famous. Prrraah!

'The Emperor froze and, taking up the ostrich head which had been retrieved for him by one of his helpers, he strode across to where the offending report had come from. Very close to where I was sitting, as it happened. No well-bred man knows how to make a noise like that even if he wants to, so I am sure that none of my companions were guilty, but it was still towards the balcony of us Senators that the Emperor came. I froze too.

'He said nothing, but his meaning was not hard to guess. He spat, and I felt the spray of his spittle reach my cheek. Then he gibbered like a monkey. Then he raised his fist with the lopped-off ostrich head in it and shook it at us, as much as to say, "One more comment of the kind, and this is what I will do to the lot of you!" (And though the spittle washed off, I have an ostrich bloodstain on my best sandals to this day to prove that what I am saying is true.) And then he laughed his high, madman's laugh and turned away.

'As he left us, two rows of senators toppled from their benches out of sheer fright, bringing me to the ground with them, and in the confusion which resulted in setting things to rights again, I and two or three others of my build saw our chance for escape and took it, crawling out from under the tangle of legs and benches on our stomachs. And that is the magnificent Indoor Hunt for you, Galen, as I remember it.'

MONSTRUM HORRENDUM, INFORME, INGENS . . .

(Or full-length portrait of a Monster.)

S o, no, my task with my chosen historian is not going to be an easy one, that much is clear now. To keep my vehicle going in the right direction I will have to drive it like a hot-head Jew. Fortunately, Cassius has seen little, but what little he has seen has come to him through the distorting medium of fear and prejudice, and it will be hard indeed for me to remove this filter for him and get him to see true. The Emperor Nero, being extremely short-sighted, is said to have watched the games from preference through the boss of a large skew-shaped emerald which had the property of bringing things closer to the viewer while at the same time elongating them and turning them unavoidably green; Cassius for his part seems to have watched them through a ruby or a garnet, or a stone at any rate, that has stained all the objects in his field of vision with a deep senatorial purple.

His description of the Hunt is sincere, of course, and that is the crux of the trouble. It is a sincere account, made by a sincere man, in full possession of his faculties at the time, neither drunk nor drowsy nor inattentive (indeed, in view of the fact that he already had it in mind to write about what he saw afterwards, Cassius as a spectator was probably more attentive than most). And yet for all its sincerity it contains only one statement that I myself am prepared to endorse as being in any way correct, and that is the first, namely that the month was August. Everything else, from quite simple things such as the colour of the awnings and the light and temperature inside the arena, down to the more complex such as the mood of the public and the nature of their applause, is – not falsehood, no, that would be an easier fault to come to grips with – but the product of what for want of a better word I can only call illusion on the part of the observer.

It is not the right moment, though, for me to deliver a lecture on optics: for that I need to make preparation. Nor do I see much advantage to be gained at this stage in taking the Senator to task over the many inaccuracies which his description contains. His mind, ruby-glazed though it is, is my last hope now and I must treat it with every regard. No shocks to it, no tugs, just a gentle, coaxing pressure. The charting operation which Marcus recommended is so far discouraging? It is indeed, it is enough to flatten a rainbow. But never mind, having taken it thus far I must finish it and know the worst.

So instead of quibbling, I thank my noble patient for granting me this very personal reminiscence of the Emperor ('and such a vivid one, Excellency, too. I could almost fancy myself back in the tribunes'), and go on to ask from what other sources the relevant chapter in his History is to be drawn – apart, that is, from direct observation, which as he himself admits was rather scant?

There is a silence, and the Senator's voice when it comes sounds surprised, almost offended. What do I mean, he asks, what sources? He is not writing about the remote past that he needs sources, he is writing about things that took place during his own lifetime. Things he – well, not witnessed exactly, if I want to put that tight a bridle on certainty, but things he *knows*.

'Yes, Excellency,' I say. 'Of course. But when I speak of sources, I do not in the least intend to dispute Your Excellency's knowledge, merely to discover how it came about.'

Ah, says Cassius, mollified, but not greatly. Well, how *does* knowledge of current events come about? In the usual way, he supposes: friends, connections, the habit of moving in the right circles and keeping one's wits about one. Letters too; yes, letters are important. He has never really given much thought to the matter, but he thinks that is the way it is: part accident of birth, part ability, part just the blessing of having a lively and enquiring mind and plenty of influential friends. A man in his position does not have to dig for his information amongst stacks of parchment and records, I must realize, like some petty clerk in an office; it comes to him naturally, like the air he breathes.

Breathing in knowledge through the nostrils? The method is new to me. 'And your father's consulship?' I ask – concealing a trap in my question, for I know for a fact that old Cassius Apronianus during his entire tenure never set so much as his big toe within the palace gates. 'Wouldn't that have been some help to you in this case as well?'

But Cassius's honesty needs no ulterior testing, it is greater even than I hoped. 'My father's consulship,' he says, 'taught me to add unapproachability to the Emperor's other defects. It taught me little else – save that it was a mistake on my father's part ever to accept the tenure. I know his motives were good, but the results were not. He was made a fool of by the Emperor and courtiers alike, poor man, and he got nothing out of the office but worry and humiliation and shame.'

Not quite exact, although I am sure Cassius believes it to be so. By my reckoning, not only did Apronianus, like all the other consuls, know from the outset that the post was purely nominal, but he also received a large sum of money for lending his name and keeping out of the way. However, this is not the sort of thing you tell your son, and not the sort of thing a son likes to hear.

So I return to the question of the Emperor's defects, which is where I need to be anyway, and ask the Senator if he would mind giving me a somewhat fuller account of these while we are on the subject. At this Cassius laughs, and says that if I want a really full account then I must wait until the chapter is written and published as it will be all defects from beginning to end. If I like, though, he adds, he could show me in the meantime the preparatory notes on which the chapter is to be based: they too are defects from beginning to end.

Showing them to me would serve little purpose, I reply – sternly, because I wish to put an end to the laughter – but if His Excellency would be so gracious as to read them out to me, then I would appreciate it indeed.

And this His Excellency duly does. Realizing immediately the extreme importance of this document in so far as the planning of my strategy is concerned, I ask to be given a copy. My request is granted, and it is this copy that I here reproduce. The asterisks, incidentally, are not Cassius's but mine, added by my secretary for convenience's sake to indicate those things and events which the Senator witnessed – or thought he witnessed – with his own senses. As with the description of the Hunt, it is the close but at the same time utterly wrong-headed relation to the truth which constitutes the biggest stumbling-block. If, as I imagine, it is Severus in person who is responsible for the distortion, then he has done his work well. Absurdities there are, of course, and plenty. For example, I deny the foul breath; I never noticed that the shadow was any different from the next man's; I think the tales of the midwife's finger and the throttling in the cradle are nonsense (but then as you will note so too does Cassius); I am uncertain about the episode of the 'Bath-water'; do not even know what is meant by that of the 'Dwarves Smeared in Mustard'; and I have several reserves about the theories of conception as well, but apart from these cavils, all of them fairly minor, I have no solid, factual objections to raise that I have not raised already. Not even about the death of Marcus. These things happened. They did not happen quite as Cassius says they did, but they happened and there is no escaping it. And now for the text.

PREPARATORY NOTES FOR A CHARACTER-PORTRAYAL OF THE DECEASED EMPEROR LUCIUS AELIUS COMMODUS ANTONINUS – COMMONLY KNOWN AS THE ENEMY OF ALL MANKIND, OR, MORE SIMPLY, THE MONSTER:

CONCEPTION (runs the first heading, because the Senator is methodical and observes strict chronological order)

VERSION (i) Commodus's mother was flighty but innocuous; his father, the closest approximation to perfection that mankind has ever expressed. Evil developed in the child through the unfortunate positioning of the stars at the moment of fecundation, and a consequent gathering of all negative influences in one foetus, all good in the other.

VERSION (ii) His mother was a whore. He and his twin brother were sired on her not by her husband, the Emperor Marcus Aurelius, but by one of her many lovers – a gladiator of brutish nature and aspect from whom they inherited their taints. The other twin dying in infancy, in his case the defects never became apparent.

VERSION (iii) His mother was a whore, but whores too lie with their husbands from time to time, thus the actual father of the twins was indeed the Emperor Marcus Aurelius. Taints to the foetuses, particularly to that situated in the lower part of the womb (i.e. Commodus), were incurred later, thanks to the

38

Empress Faustina's repeated and wanton coupling with a gladiator during the advanced stages of her pregnancy. Semen, sweat, and simple pressure are variously cited as vehicles of transmission.

VERSION (iv) As above. The variant being that the Empress Faustina repented of her infatuation with the fighter, confessed to her husband, and allowed herself to be persuaded by the Palace Priests to have her lover slain and to take a purifying bath in his blood, still warm. In this case the contaminating agent is unnamed, but is presumably to be identified in the blood itself, entering the womb by misadventure and/or prolonged immersion.

'These,' (Cassius reminds himself punctually in a note to his notes) 'the four most accredited versions of genesis. Assess carefully before deciding which to use. Each, indeed all, may well be true: there is no logical conflict, that is, or not so far as I can see, in asserting both that the stars were aligned against Commodus from the start, *and* that he was begotten by a gladiator, *and* battered by a gladiator while still in the womb (the same man or another, it makes little difference), and later, still in the womb, yet *further* tainted by drops of the gladiator's blood. On the contrary, the strength of such an explanation can only be appealing to the writer.

'But strength and logic are not everything, and what perhaps merits paramount consideration is whether or not the charge of Marcus Aurelius's cuckoldry is not almost worse, from the point of view of his dignity, than the one it is introduced to eliminate. Assess, therefore, and re-assess until sure.'

BIRTH: Heavily unpropitious. Heralded by negative portents – two earth tremors in the centre of the peninsula, and a blood-red rainstorm in the south; difficult, as twin births nearly always are; and marred by the immediate discovery of grave disfigurement★ to one of the infant's bodies, namely that of Commodus. Allegedly, the midwife in attendance, seeing the deformity, tried to prevent the new-born child from drawing its first breath and was rewarded for her pains by having her finger bitten off. Even if true, however, this anecdote smacks of slaves' gossip and the kitchen. Do not use.

INFANCY: Warped and hapless. The second physical deformity★ made its appearance at this time. Both twins sickly, as all Marcus

Aurelius's male children were (Commodus being the only one to achieve manhood), and both on more than one occasion on the threshold of death. Whether or not the infant Commodus helped his brother over the threshold by throttling him in the cradle which they shared, in view of the fact of his delicate state of health at the time, must be open to doubt. Certain, however, is that one twin died and that the other returned from this brush with the underworld afflicted for life with malodorous breath and a particularly dense quality of shadow – black where other men's are grey★. Marcus Aurelius is said to have commented on his loss with the words, 'I am deprived of my lion cub and left with the jackal'. Apocryphal or not, relating to this death or that of another son a little later on, the phrase deserves quoting as it gives a very good idea of the way the poor man must have felt.

CHILDHOOD: Already scandalous. Cite in illustration the schoolroom fiasco and the horrifying episode of the Bath-water. Ignore, however, on the same grounds as the story of the midwife's finger, reports of lesser faults such as the child's irrepressible tendency to dance, whistle, use coarse language, take frequent baths, whistle while *in* the bath, and mould clay pots instead of attending to his lessons. A historian is sometimes obliged to descend very low, but his place is not in the mire.

YOUTH: Less is known of this period of Commodus's life than any other. Being still under the restraining influence of his father, it would seem that no outright atrocities were committed at this stage, save for the debauch of one of his sisters. Which sister, it is hard to discover with accuracy, but I think it fairly safe to presume it was Lucilla, the one he later murdered. Handle this point, however, with due reserve.

EARLY MANHOOD: Period marked by the death of Marcus Aurelius and a subsequent loosening of the reins with all that entails. Query: did Commodus *really* murder his own father when they were on campaign together on the northern front? The charge is so grave that I think it should not be voiced by the historian unless completely certain. What can and should be voiced, however, is our young ruler's despicable behaviour at this time in general, and the appallingly inept inaugural speech to the Senate★ with which he marked the beginning of his reign.

MATURITY: Refer back to own chapter on Marcus Aurelius and contrast point by point. Use opening metaphor of stately tree on the one hand and on the other of weed or poisonous plant growing to huge and terrible proportions, suffocating all that surrounds it; or else metaphor taken from metallurgy – gold versus rusty iron; or else from animal kingdom – owl and vulture, lion and jackal (no, not lion and jackal, that has been used already by Marcus, but something of the kind). Then on to policies, or lack of them. And finally, the atrocities proper. Be sparing of these, however, and leave the worst of them to petty chroniclers. Mention the brothel, for example, but not the goings-on which took place inside it. Mention the tortures, but do not name them singly. Say nothing of the unfortunate fat man, nor of the 'Dwarves Smeared in Mustard', and leave out the famous but utterly repugnant episode known as 'The Bird and the Worms'. Include, on the other hand, however repugnant, one or more of the stories relating to sacrilege, such as 'The Mithraic Murder', 'The Desecration of the Rites of Isis', 'The Virgin and the Pinecones', etc., since Commodus's attitude to religion is important. Lastly, list the outrages committed publically in the arena in the grips of the closing bout of madness and give one example of these (the Hunt★) in detail. And then pass with relief to:

DEATH: Here give straightforward official version, minus the tittle-tattle. And:

DELETION FROM PUBLIC MEMORY: List measures, commend and close.

PART III

THE DEFENCE

DESINIT IN PISCEM

(From Horace: It ends in a fish-tail, i.e. deteriorates, ends badly.)

Nurses' stories for children are full of good personages, tripping around in white dresses with stars on their foreheads and rosebuds in their mouths, and bad ones, clad in rags and spitting toads and pomice. As a child, I admit I myself found the idea of people vomiting flowers every bit as worrying as that of people vomiting reptiles, but that is not the point; the point is that the good characters were characterized in a particular, very recognizable way, and the evil characters likewise.

And stories for adults are not very different when you come to think of it: whatever his foibles may have been in real life, for the chroniclers, a good ruler is nearly always a grave, stern man, studious and frugal, merciful in peace, merciless in war, has a high forehead, well-arched feet and a noble carriage, speaks like an orator, and showers presents on his people, whether they deserve them or not, whether he can afford it or not. Whereas a bad ruler is coarse, vain, mean towards others and indulgent with himself, low-browed, flat-footed, gruff-voiced, illiterate, preferably mad as well, and conducts himself on the battlefield with the valour of a rabbit on the run.

Some of the more stylized and conventional anecdotes in circulation regarding Commodus do not therefore trouble me overmuch because I feel that time itself will do them justice. Is it possible, I am confident that readers will begin to ask themselves in years to come, that *all* wicked Emperors kept a slave with a gigantic member on which they bestowed kisses? That they *all* gave lascivious names to their minions? *All* possessed a favourite horse to which they fed thrushes' eggs and honey? *All* prowled the city by night stabbing passers-by and visiting the brothels? *All* dressed themselves up like harlots and minced and preened and cleaned their backsides after defecation on day-old chicks? Didn't some of them, evil though they may have been, have different vices? And haven't the writers been perhaps a little lazy in describing them all in this colourful, yes, but after a while, somewhat flat and uniform way? Isn't it time we started to take these accusations with a grain of salt?

So much, then, for the hundreds of run-of-the-mill anecdotes on the lips of all today as yesterday. Unfortunately, though, as far as their rebuttal is concerned, the charges which Cassius brings against Commodus in his notes are not of this kind at all. Far from it, they are, as I said, at least from a strictly factual point of view, uncomfortably close to the truth. Because Cassius is not a mere chronicler, he is a genuine historian, and Severus is most definitely not a nurse. My task is therefore not to attempt to deny the charges, but to present them to my listener under a different light. *Not* the angry sensational purple glow which his upbringing and training have accustomed him to view them in, but the clear, transparent light of fairness and reason.

And since this process will necessarily involve the removal of his ruby spy-glass of which he is no doubt very fond, and must thus be carried out slowly, stealthily, almost imperceptibly, if he is not to realize what is happening and grab hold of the glass again all the more tightly, I think it wise on my next visit to the Senator to grant him another little dose of freedom and to let him choose the topic of our next discussion.

Cassius is no fool, of course. He cannot perhaps yet see the exact destination I want to lead him to, but he can guess the direction well enough and does not greatly relish taking it. He is prompt in his reply. If the choice lies with him, he says, then of all the items on the list, the one he would like to hear me speak about first, always from my singular doctor's angle, is the worst and most widely observed of all the atrocities, the notorious 'Massacre of the Cripples'. He received the news of it himself in a letter from a fellow-senator in the following terms (and he reads from the letter, which I notice he has ready to hand):

'Last week, you may be interested to hear, our fond Prince excelled himself. He caused to be assembled together all the men in the city who had lost their feet as a result of disease or some accident, and then, after fastening about their knees some likenesses of serpents' bodies, and giving them sponges to throw instead of stones, killed them with the blows of a club, pretending that they were giants. A pretty solution. The city is purged of its lame inhabitants, and the sound are kept amused and made to gape.'

Cassius leaves it unvoiced, but the implication behind his choice is clear: 'There, explain *that* to me, my good Galen, and you can explain anything.' So I try to do just this. Although it is far from easy.

The great mock Sea-Battle – for I assume this is the event which Cassius's correspondent refers to – took place exactly one year before the hunt, and together with it, and several other slightly smaller but still very novel and spectacular displays, formed an important, one might almost say a culminating part of Commodus's overall political strategy. (Strategy which I begin now cautiously to outline for my listener's benefit, but desist when I sense his alarm. To Cassius, the masses, like flies, are an oversight of Nature – pesky, abundant, and serving no discernable purpose. A ruler has no business to extend a hand to them, therefore, unless it is prudently equipped with a swatter. Why should an Emperor want to know the rabble of which the vast majority of his subjects is composed? Why should he want this rabble to know him? What good could spring from such an acquaintance? Whom could it benefit? What purpose could it serve? Baffling, incomprehensible questions undeserving of an answer.) The reign being already in its eleventh year, my voluntary eclipse was almost accomplished by then and had been so for some while. Thus, although I was amongst those who helped shape the strategy when it was little more than a vague idea in Commodus's mind, I had no hand at all in its realization, and during this, as indeed all the other occasions of its kind, I sat in my seat in the crowd and watched like any other spectator.

Did the loss of my post as Court Physician rankle with me? Cassius wants to know here, anxious to return to the ground that is more familiar to him. I reply, quite truthfully, that it did not. Because it was not loss, it was spontaneous retirement. I minded a little that it should be *thought* that I minded, I tell him, but the wound to my pride went no deeper than that. A lifetime of teaching has shown me that the pupil to rejoice over is not the docile one who remains to rinse out the flasks for you, but the one who cuts himself loose – even kicking you on the shins as he does so – and sets up his own practice. And although in the case of Commodus it was I, if anyone, who had done the kicking, it couldn't but please me to see him free of all mentors at last and going his own way. At this, Cassius sucks in a breath of disapproval – men of his class submit to their mentors even at ninety – but makes no comment.

I return to my story. Without gusto but without much trouble either, because like the Condemnation this is another unwelcome memory which keeps all its primitive burnish. The battle was staged in the Flavian amphitheatre – a building which to me has always seemed to possess the remarkable quality of being huge when it is empty, and cramped when it is full, but never the same size and never the right one. Its central cavity had been staunched and then flooded for the occasion to yield a surface which again tended to veer unhappily between large and small, lake and puddle, but which today, thanks to the great number of rafts and platforms which had been set afloat on it, came closer to the puddle.

The depth of the water was congruous, less than a foot throughout. This was officially announced as a safety-measure: so that families, that is, could feel free to send their children to splash about in the water during the weeks of preparation without fear of their drowning (a drowned child being a bad omen for the success of the spectacle, and a drowned cat worse). But I think there may have been a technical reason for it as well. For Commodus's purpose, you see, for this marriage of theatre and arena which he was trying to achieve on so unprecedented a scale, verisimilitude was an essential factor. And since real-life snakes rear vertical only at the moment of attack and for the rest of the time move on their bellies, it may well have been that he wanted his own snakes to do the same, and that the only way he could make sure that they did so was by keeping the water-level to an absolute minimum. But this is only a guess; I do not know for sure.

What I do know for sure, though, is that despite what is implied in Cassius's letter, the contest did not consist in the one-sided killing of unarmed men got up to resemble some form of water-serpent – apart from anything else it would have been unthinkable to serve such

48

crude entertainment to the connoisseur audience of the capital – but, in intention at least, in a two-sided and evenly matched encounter between Giants on the one hand and Sea-Snakes on the other. Or, to be more exact, between a team of professional fighters dressed as giants, and a team dressed as serpents.

The political implications behind this choice of contestants were not made explicit, since, as I said, the fight was originally planned as a fair one and its outcome must therefore have been uncertain, but I think it reasonable to assume (and just as reasonable *not* to divulge to Cassius at this stage) that the snakes were tacitly intended, especially if they lost, to represent members of the Senate.

As regards the programme, it was uniform: there was the fight, that is, on the grandest scale imaginable, and there was nothing else, neither to open the proceedings nor to close them. A measure, this, almost certainly introduced in the interests of decorum by eliminating the scrappy 'warming-up' bouts which normally precede the main event and the even scrappier which follow, and as such laudable. But also very unfortunate, as it meant that when the hitch occurred there was no way of distracting the crowd's attention or of filling in the time. What the hitch was due to exactly, I learnt only later. At the time, after a two-hour wait and no public announcement to placate them, many of the spectators had devised rival battles of their own, and there was no way of telling anything, except that things were wrong and would soon be wronger still. Afterwards, however, I was told that it was simply this: that at the very last moment, when the engaged teams went into their dressing-rooms to prepare for the encounter, they discovered that the costumes for the snakes – tight-fitting tubes or sheaths designed to encase the lower part of the body like the tail of a siren – had been (accidentally? purposely? who can say?) sewn so tight that no member of the team could get into them. With the result that there was this long, awkward interval while the ball of responsibility was tossed from seamsters to outfitters to armourers to impresarios and back again, and unsuccessful attempts were made to enlarge the sheaths, and more were ordered to replace them and none came, and so on for the best part of the morning.

One person I spoke to, mind you, did have a slightly different explanation to offer. According to him, the delay was due, not to the botched measurements of the costumes, but to a downright refusal on the part of the fighters to wear them. The entire team, he said, had rebelled as soon as they saw the tails, realizing how severely these would hamper their movements, and had sat down on the spot in porcupine formation, spears in hand, shouting that they had been tricked, and that if they were to die they would prefer to do so as men and not as serpents; and nothing, neither threats nor promises of higher pay to their families had managed to make them change their minds. But I do not believe the story myself. For one thing it is trite and I have heard it already in other contexts, and for another I have worked too long with professional fighters and their managers not to know that the conditions of combat are always laid down very carefully beforehand to avoid just this sort of inconvenience. Since when, too, are weapons handed out in the dressing-rooms, I would like to know? That would be asking for trouble.

But anyway, apart from the fact that it was trivial and unforeseen, the reason for the delay is not important: delay there undeniably was, and a very long and dangerous one, and Commodus's decision on how to remedy matters before the crowd lost its patience altogether, as I try to impress upon Cassius, must be seen in this light. 'A dark light', is his only comment.

Yes, Excellency, a dark light. But, as I remind him, leadership is not for the squeamish and not for the hesitant either, and he must bear in mind that much, much more was at stake than the success of the manifestation itself. I will openly confess to him, I say, that I have often since asked myself whether I would have acted in quite the same way as the Emperor had I been in a similar position, and that my answer has always tended to be no, that I would not. But I think this is because the question itself is ill-formulated: the fact is that when I have been in a *comparable* position – not a similar one, mark him well, which is quite different, but a comparable one – I too have acted swiftly and ruthlessly and have privileged what I have judged at that instant to be the greater good. Leg or gangrene? Mother or child? Knife or life? It is not always easy to decide such things correctly; it is not always easy to see whether or not a correct decision exists: all that *can* be seen is the need to make a decision of some kind before it is too late.

And whatever else may be said of it, Commodus's decision did at least have the merit of being made – just – in time. The solution he hit on was a simple and practical one and says much for the often disputed logicality of his mind. Were the costumes essential? he must have reasoned, or could they be jettisoned and ordinary fighting gear be used in their stead? They were essential: the arena was full of water, the water was prepared for snakes, the public was expecting snakes – indeed clamouring for them by now – and snakes they would have to have. To obtain real snakes or indeed any other kind of water animal was out of the question at such short notice; therefore, imitation snakes it had to be. New costumes could not be provided? They could not be provided. (Well, that is to say they *could* presumably be provided but the thing would take time. Proper measurements would have to be taken, the material would need cutting and tacking and fitting; and then would come the actual sewing; and the tails were long, and the material was thick, and the stitches in order to hold had to be small and close together, so that in all likelihood by the time the sewers had finished, with the public in its present mood there would be more need for shrouds than for fancy costumes.) Then, seeing that this was how things stood, there was only one thing for it: a new team of fighters must be found on the instant, sufficiently slim to fit into the costumes.

So Commodus's mind must have worked, and so must he have arrived at his idiosyncratic solution. Despite the ban, many stories (and just as many absurdities) have been told about the way he put the solution into practice, criticism being levelled in particular against the way he set about recruiting his substitute team. Some versions, like the one in Cassius's letter, suggest that there was a hasty round-up of maimed and crippled individuals throughout the city; others state that the round-up was conducted within the precincts of the amphitheatre itself; others go further and say that able-bodied people were purposely maimed on the spot – cut down to size, as it were, and stuffed summarily into the costumes like flowers into a vase; others still accuse Commodus of having carried out this task himself: chop, chop, chop, stuff, stuff, stuff, with a smile on his face the while. All of them in some form or another cite the coercion of non-professional elements on the basis of bodily size alone.

Now, naturally I would like to be able to assure Cassius straight out that there is no truth in any of these tales, but honesty must be met with honesty, and I cannot in conscience do so. The public sector of the amphitheatre was in a state of near turmoil by the time the battle started, and although I think it unlikely that conscription was actually carried out from among the spectators – on the grounds of safety if nothing else – I cannot exclude it from what I saw.

Certainly Commodus did not perform this task himself, that charge is clearly ludicrous, and certainly there was no extemporary maiming of the sound, for how could such men be expected to fight so soon afterwards? But it is indeed possible that in order to make up numbers a few suitable individuals were cropped from the ranks of the general populace, just as it is possible, given the haste, that these last-minute replacements were in some cases introduced into their costumes without much ceremony.

I say *possible* to Cassius, but I am afraid I really mean that it was likely. Likely, at any rate, that if not these then there were other, equally grave irregularities. The battle when it finally got under way was confused to the point of chaos and reminded me of nothing so much as an overturned tank of eels set upon by hungry cats, so here again I was able to see very little. However, despite the splashing and the flailing and the cover afforded by the tails, I am bound to admit that I caught sight of at least three members of the snake team bearing heavy physical handicaps: one totally legless man (who as it happened fought very adroitly and may therefore have simply been what is called in the trade an 'acorn' – a wounded professional, that is, who from the severity of his wounds has become expendable and thus in the eyes of his trainers fit only for pig-fodder), and two others with what looked to be amputations of the leg at roughly thigh-level, although not recent ones.

In itself, of course, the presence of such disabled fighters is not very significant: it could simply mean, as I said, that in order to make up his team Commodus tapped the reserves of the 'acorns', or that he threw in the odd prisoner or two, or both. Indeed, this is probably what he did. But it takes on a more disturbing aspect when coupled with another detail which came to my attention a little later on: namely, when I saw two more members of the snake formation – whether invalids or not I could not tell, but they definitely looked very undersized to me and very scrawny – crawl to the edge of the arena where a barrier of rocks had been erected, and, one after the other, beat their heads against the rocks until they were senseless. This is not – or not normally – the behaviour of any class of professional fighter, 'acorns' included, for whom resistance is a matter of honour. Nor is it the behaviour of non-professionals enlisted on regular terms, since in their case it would lead to the forfeiture of all compensation money to kindred. Still less is it the behaviour of hardened criminals. It is the behaviour of men in utter despair.

I do not think it necessary to mention much of this to Cassius, especially not the bit about the attempted suicides, as there is such a thing as an overdose of truth. But I make no secret of the conclusion I draw from it, which is this: that although Commodus's reluctance to do so must have been great, and although I am sure he tried all the normal channels of recruitment first and only resorted to force when these had failed, nevertheless the team of 'Sea-Snakes' that he finally sent into the arena was indeed composed, at least in part, of conscripted individuals of non-professional status and less than robust build.

But, I urge Cassius to consider, but. Is this to be termed the action of a human monster, or can it not better be seen as the action of a responsible ruler, placed in an extremely difficult situation? How many men did the Emperor sacrifice unjustly? Let us say twenty, thirty, fifty at the most. How many would have died had the riot in the arena broken out as it threatened to do? Hundreds for sure. To say nothing of the shipwreck of Commodus's policy and the dire consequences that would almost certainly have ensued. Was the solution he adopted, therefore, so very cruel after all? Or was it not – ruthless to be sure, but in its curious way correct, even humane? We are, after all, talking about poor-quality human material. (Perhaps because I am still not entirely happy in my mind about the episode I try to speak here with all the conviction I can muster, but my voice is robbed of some of its firmness by the sudden intrusive vision of Marcus – not *my* Marcus, but the grim, bitter, sepulchral Marcus of the last period – warning me against just this: the counting of men as if they were heads of cattle. I blot out the vision immediately, though, because the latter-day Marcus has already caused me quite enough trouble as it is.)

Cassius is silent. I can hear him scratching his head, doing his arithmetic. More stories first, he says, please, before he commits himself to an answer. More stories and more massage. He would like to hear what I have to say about the 'Mithraic Murder', for example. Yes, now we are on the subject of the great public outrages he would like to hear how I intend to give an in-any-way-plausible account of that one.

POST FATA RESURGO

(After death – if you smite me in the right place –
I will rise again.)

C assius probably thinks to corner me with this choice of his, but in fact I am glad that he has singled out a topic connected with religion. Because Commodus's attitude towards religion was, as the Senator himself remarks in his notes, although perhaps with rather a different meaning from my own, important. Important because religion itself was ever faster becoming an important force to be reckoned with on the political scene, and important because Commodus – far better than Marcus, far, far better than myself – was able to appreciate this fact and to shape his actions accordingly.

Why this should have been so I do not know for certain, but I suspect it had something to do with involvement. Or with passion, if you prefer. A cool head, detachment, is traditionally supposed to give one an advantage in the shepherding of others; so much so that the most reputable schools recommend that a leader, or would-be leader, shun not only wine and beer and copulation and gambling and hunting, but indeed any form of excitement whatever down to that innocuous pastime that is mouse-racing. Marcus believed this – there were no harnessed mice allowed in the nursery, you can be sure – and for a while I believed it myself. But I have since come to think that the doctrine is mistaken, and to understand that just as heat draws in medicine, so heat draws in love, and heat draws in every other sphere of human activity, politics included. Heat, passion and involvement – three thin but mysteriously strong traces with which you can hitch any number of wagons to your yoke and see them roll. Are not the best cooks always greedy? Do not the most successful seducers truly love their quarry – at least until they have caught it? Does the discerning collector not follow his heart in preference to his head when choosing a new item to add to his store? And – I am not quite so sure about this one, but I will try it all the same – are not the really great storytellers always the first to believe their own stories?

Marcus and I were strangers to religious sentiment, religious fervour – in our different ways of course: Marcus more regretful, I more secure and dismissive. We could see that it existed, we could see its strength and what could be done with it – I can remember Marcus, for instance, stretching out his fingers once and saying, 'There is a soft spot in nearly every man's head, Galen, where he keeps his idols, cushioned so as not to break them. And like the bull's muzzle, grasp hold of this soft spot and you can lead him where you will'. But we had never really felt the presence of this vulnerable zone inside our own frames, either of us, and this meant that we did not either of us fully understand its workings, nor know quite where it was placed, nor how to reach it. Marcus said the head, I thought myself that it was in the genitals or in the feet inasmuch as what devotees of most sects seemed to me to be after was either wild stimulation or else license to plod along obediently in the steps of their ancestors; both of us were wrong.

Commodus, though, was made of different stuff altogether, and when he judged that the moment was ripe for this kind of extension to his policy – after the bleeding of the monied classes, that is, when he had, so to speak, chopped all his sticks to more or less the same length through continuous taxation, and before the final phase of religious and political unification in which all the sticks were to be bound tightly into one great bundle under his sole charge – he unerringly put his finger on the correct spot of his subjects' anatomy: their hearts, and began to exert the right amount of pressure.

This is not to say that he knew instinctively which cult to make use of: he did not, and the episodes which are cited in Cassius's notes as the 'Mithraic Murder' or the 'Virgin and the Pinecones' and so forth were in fact part of his way of finding out. But, unlike Marcus who thought it was sufficient to pop all the various denominations together into a kind of cauldron and allow people to pick out the one they liked, Commodus knew that what was needed was one, unique cult to the exclusion of all others. And knew too, within a certain radius, which sort of cult it had to be.

He must have spent – what would it have been? – nine months, perhaps ten, a fair period of gestation anyway, in what he called his 'explorative' phase, before passing to the conclusive. And this being the time when my services were still needed and I was still very much in his confidence, I accompanied him on several of his trickier missions. Most of them, naturally, pertaining to the latter phase, when his mind was made up and it was only a question of bringing exposure and discredit on the cults which had been discarded. It was often handy for him, I think, to have a doctor in tow at such times. Thus, I was present at the Mithraic mockery (or the first of the Mithraic mockeries, because others were later ordered in the same pattern for the provinces, and in total more than a score must have been carried out); I was present at the 'Deflowering' or 'De-coning' of the Virgin (or again the first of the series of 'De-conings'); and I was present, although not as a doctor this time but as a simple spectator, at the Isis Festival, where I can remember getting stomach cramps at one point of the proceedings so hard did I laugh.

I could therefore, I suppose, explain all these episodes singly to Cassius if he wanted, but I think (and assure him that he also will think when he has heard me out) that the one he has chosen is quite enlightening enough. As I point out to him, in all cases the Emperor's intent was much the same, so were the methods he adopted, and so too were the methods of the calumniators in concocting their stories afterwards. If His Excellency wishes, therefore, just by changing a few details here and there and replacing swords by pinecones and truncheons, and youths with maidens and so forth, he can then sort out the others for himself.

It is possible of course, I admit frankly before I start, that in some of the subsequent operations – not those performed by the Emperor in person, but those carried out on his instructions – things did not always go so smoothly and that there were cases of abuse. Perhaps not *very* dissimilar to those reported, although I doubt on physiological grounds that the alleged number of pinecones could ever be introduced into a human vagina. This, however, I remind Cassius firmly, is a different matter, having to do with military discipline, and not one that need concern us here. (And quickly, before Marcus's spectre has time to put in another accusing appearance – for what was it he said to me that evening as he lay there crouched in that terrible foetal position which he assumed more and more frequently towards the end? 'Everything must concern us, Galen, everything and everybody.

Even this tiny ant here which crawls across the palm of my hand' – I go ahead with my explanation.)

I have promised Cassius it will be enlightening, but enlightening is of course a very ill-chosen word to use when speaking of Mithras and his benighted followers. I have never known such darkness as enfolded Commodus and myself when the last curtain was drawn aside for us and we were admitted into the seventh and innermost sanctum: I felt as if my eyes had been put out and replaced by two little stumps of charcoal. I tended to agree with Marcia that a cult like this – that is, which idolized Time, which I so abhor, which excluded women whom I do not abhor, and which packed its worshippers into dank underground spaces as if they were a colony of luckless moles – hardly deserved our consideration.

Commodus, though, was of a more lenient opinion and had been so all along. He was on what must, I think, have been his twelfth or thirteenth visit – a fully official one this time, his identity declared and everyone bowing and scraping and coming forward with perfumes and special scarves and slippers and whatnots to protect him from the cold. And although, unknown to our hosts, it was to be a visit of rejection, the mere fact that it had taken him so long to decide which side to come down on shows how keen his interest was in the activities of this particular sect and how sincere his intentions during the phase of flirtation and courtship.

I use the metaphor of wooing advisedly, because in our search for a suitable creed the Emperor, his confidante and myself did indeed behave not unlike a trio of seneschals in the marriage market. Each time we came upon a promising candidate, that is, we would take her and consider her written credentials first – her descent, her contacts, her allegiances, whom she could be counted on to bring with her and whom not, whom the union would please and whom antagonize and so forth. Then, still keeping our distance, we would review her morals and appearance and carriage and the company she kept. And finally, this done, we would step forward and begin to observe her for ourselves at close range. Anxious, like the matchmakers to find – yes, grace and beauty and appeal, but above all signs of fertility and docility and readiness to adapt to her new station.

Apart from its hostility to women, which, unlike Marcia and me, Commodus thought a minor matter and one that could soon be rectified, Mithraism had passed the first test remarkably well. It was a movement on the crest of a wave, its followers were numerous and growing all the time. They came from all walks of life, but the inner hierarchy seemed in no way to reflect social standing or even wealth, so that among the two uppermost categories – the 'Fathers', as I think they were called, and the 'Sun-Messengers' or 'Sun-Runners' – there were to be found greengrocers and pedlars and simple foot-soldiers and even slaves, while at the other end of the scale, in the ranks of what were inexplicably called the 'Crows' there were aristocrats and generals and powerful businessmen. And this mingling of the orders we all three of us thought an excellent thing: if religion was to bring solace to the dispossessed, we agreed, it must surely offer them the possibility of some form of advancement, be it only advancement along a dark, and downward-leading tunnel.

Another thing in the cult's favour was that there was a sturdy tradition of solidarity between members: the richer, for example, regularly and uncomplainingly funding for the poorer such services as free coaching for gifted children, free legal aid to litigate, free treatment for the sick, and even, when this last had proved vain, free burial. It meant of course that the association was tight-knit and that much harder to penetrate as a result, but even so we thought that once it *had* been penetrated the tradition would provide a good base for further development. We did not delude ourselves that the match, if clinched, would be widely popular, but we felt that what breadth of popularity it did achieve would be sufficient, and could be widened without difficulty later – principally through bringing in the women.

This, our first estimate, made from afar. Our second viewing, made from the middle distance, was, if anything, more encouraging still. Especially to Commodus, who, as I said, had a better feel for these things than I. (Marcia remained scornful, but then she had a right to be. And besides, by then I think she had already set her eyes elsewhere.)

The rites – what could be learnt of them at this remove – seemed to be just what we were looking for: a blend of dignity and savagery in proportions designed to uplift but not tire. They were organized in a kind of spiral movement. First, there was the usual bland Washing Ceremony for neophytes in which everyone congregated somewhat sheepishly in the first of the seven chambers of the shrine with herbs stuck behind their ears and exchanged gifts and kisses. This was followed by a series of trials and privations of varying intensity conducted at varying levels of depth within the shrine (and the deeper the location, naturally, the tougher the trial). And finally, there came a very secret and very sacred meal for full-blown initiates, consumed at the seventh and most profound layer of all. This last, needless to say, being the ceremony in which the Emperor and myself were now invited to participate – he in quality of honorary priest, and I, after being whisked by special courtesy through the seven stages of initiation in two minutes flat, in quality of onlooker extraordinary – and this the ceremony which we intended to disturb.

The dogma Commodus also found very much to his taste. He liked, for instance, the idea of there being a triad of over-gods in the place of the more usual one: he said it made for flexibility, whatever he may have meant by this. He also liked – and for reasons I can better understand: whichever way you look at it Evil exists and cannot be ignored – the kindred idea of there being wicked gods as well as good ones. Added to which he admired the half-manly, half-divine status of Mithras himself: ingenious device, he said, which would help bring the deities closer to ordinary people (as if that were a desirable end for either, say I). And he not only admired but confessed himself deeply moved by the curious concept of redemption or deliverance on which the sect put such weight in its teachings.

To me this last theory had little to recommend it, it merely sounded as if Mithras, in paying a price to the gods for the souls he would eventually manage to capture, was acting like a fisherman who pays a tax to the port authorities on the size of his haul. But Commodus was convinced of its powers of attraction, and I think he was probably right: it was just I who lacked the equipment to appreciate it.

What I *was* able to appreciate, on the other hand, every bit as well as my imperial master, was the imagery: far superior to my way of thinking than that of the cult he and Marcia eventually settled for. Samples of it I had seen already, but some particularly fine ones I was now able to observe, if only fleetingly, as we were conducted through the flight of preliminary chambers and into the crypt. I noticed, for example, its magnificence only slightly marred by the stench of cow dung coming from the adjoining stables where the sacrificial beasts were housed, a huge wall-painting of the story of the Creation of the World, depicting Mithras locked in victorious combat with the mythical Bull of Plenty. What tension, what impact, and what pathos in the scene! I can see it now. The warrior's knife is raised, the throat of the bull is bent back in submission: you can almost hear the great bones in the neck as they crack. At Mithras's flank, his helpers, a serpent and a dog, rush to lap the blood before it falls to the ground and is spilt (the blood, it was explained to me, symbolizing Power and Knowledge, the dog and the serpent symbolizing I know not what). In the foreground another helper, a scorpion, latches itself on to the dying animal's testicles to imbibe the semen (i.e. Life itself), while the bull's eyes, turned towards the heavens, cast a last accusing look at the gods as if to say: 'Look at the greed of this creature into whose hands I have been delivered. He will drain me dry. He will leave nothing, respect nothing. He will run through all the gifts in a trice and leave behind him a marauded waste. Will you not reconsider your decision, deities, before it is too late?' Compare the force of this image with that pertaining to the other cult which was finally selected of an artisan god, carrying out his creation in the span of a working week and then resting in the shade like a simple bricklayer or carpenter to get his strength back, and I think you will see what I mean about superiority.

I also noticed – but *very* fleetingly this time, as the Emperor and I were hustled through what looked to be a torture chamber fitted out with all sorts of strange and ugly gadgets which I doubt we were really meant to see – a series of paintings illustrating what I imagine was the underworld. Greatly *in*ferior, these, if I may be forgiven the play on words, to anything similar we had so far encountered among the other cults, and thus much more impressive. Fatten up a spider, arm it with fangs and tusks and claws, cross it with a leper-woman well advanced in years and her disease, stuff peppercorns up its rectum to humour it, throw in a few warts as well, and you will have an idea of the Mithraic demon as it glared down on us in our transit. Commodus was so taken by the figure, incidentally, thought its function of frightening the faithful into good behaviour so useful, that later on he did his best to persuade the leader of his chosen cult to adopt it, warts and all, but I am not sure that his efforts met with much success. I visited a shrine a few years ago, before my eyes went, and noted a few demons on the wall there, but they were paltry little red hobgoblin creatures, wretched in comparison.

So. A fattish dowry, good blood, good connections, poise, virtue and character. With all these points in her favour, what then was lacking in the Mithraic bride, you will wonder, and why was the Emperor, with me at his side, out to repudiate her rather than take her to his bed forthwith?

The answer is simply that the lady did not pass the third test, that of adaptability. Parallel meetings with the sect's leaders finally revealed – and very literally – a core of granite at the centre of their association, aggravated by an unfortunate tendency on their part to cling to this core like barnacles. Did they have a written creed, we asked them? They did. Would they be willing to hand it over to us for examination? They hedged immediately. Well, in principle they said, yes. But in practice they were afraid it would be difficult because the articles of the creed were engraved on the face of a rock situated in a very secret underground location. We could, if we liked, they conceded (looking at one another dubiously here) – at least the *Emperor* could, they were not so sure about me – visit the rock and read the inscriptions on it, but only after having been fully initiated into the sect's mysteries. A prior visit, with a view to sampling, was out of the question.

The condition, of course, although he was careful not to say so, did not pose much of an obstacle to Commodus, who was savouring cults like wine at the present and had already attained nearly the level of a Sun-Trotter or whatever it was in this one, but for what he had in mind to discover, the visit was perhaps unnecessary. So, could the creed, he next asked lightly, assuming one of his most fatuous expressions and giving full rein to his stammer; could the creed – say that in the course of time it proved itself in some way unsound or insufficient – be modified in some way? Could its articles, rocky though they were, be erased or added to?

The reply was uncompromising: never. Not a line, not a letter of what was written could be altered, for all time. This was of the essence of Mithraism and by it the religion stood or fell.

Ah, was all Commodus said (and behind the fatuous expression I could see his brain spinning away busily and drawing its conclusions: representatives from the rival sect which Marcia championed so strongly had been interviewed that same morning and had very accommodatingly left copies of all their sacred texts – bundles and bundles of them – with an invitation, made to me in particular, to 'braid' them with as much logic as I liked). Ah, I see.

And see the Emperor did, and very clearly. The meeting had

taken place a week ago, and in the meantime he had made up his mind about Mithraism and devised this very pretty way of dealing with it which we were now about to employ. But, as I said, in the situation in which we had presently landed ourselves, neither he nor I could see so much as the tip of our own finger held before the nose, and this made things rather difficult in so far as the success of our undertaking was concerned.

It crossed my mind for a moment as I stood there, holding fast to my patron's cloak with one hand and rubbing at my charcoal eyes with the other in the hopes that it was not the light but they which were at fault, that our intentions had been somehow divined, and that in order to forestall any action on our part the entire ceremony was to be conducted under cover of total darkness.

Luckily, however, I was mistaken, and no sooner had the curtain swung to behind us than a voice in the blackness began to speak, announcing to us to have patience since the light-bearers were already on their way. 'We begin our sacred meal in darkness,' the voice intoned, 'in order to remind us of our condition before the deliverance. Mithras, our saviour, slew the Bull of Plenty and procured for us all the riches of the earth, but you will remember how, before opening its carcass, he was obliged to draw it by the hind legs through the long tunnel of suffering and deprivation. To commemorate this act we will now link hands with our neighbours and together we will pull.'

I took great care myself to do nothing of the kind, but from what ensued I could tell that whatever else they may have been, the faithful present in the crypt were certainly many and zealous. Commodus's cloak was torn from my hand and I heard him give a snort of what I thought was indignation but which he told me afterwards was laughter.

'Peace,' said the voice. And then, since peace was long in asserting itself, 'Peace' again. 'Enough, brethren, that is enough. The struggle is over. The tunnel lies behind us. Let us prepare ourselves to emerge into the light.'

Four brisk handclaps, and the curtain was drawn aside to admit the same number of youths carrying lamps. The youths wore blindfolds, and the oil in the lamps slopped dangerously. I had a moment's fear lest the 'Final Conflagration' of which the Mithraic doctrine makes mention were about to visit itself on us a little ahead of schedule, and kept close to the exit until I saw that the lamps had been safely placed. Then I stepped forward to inspect the scene. It was much as I had imagined it would be: a long narrow room, lined on its two longer sides by stone benches of very plain workmanship (too narrow for the faithful to sit on, although I noticed that this was what most of them were doing), and at its far end, set very high up so that the exact gestures of the officiant would be hard to observe, an altar block, again, in barest stone, against which were propped three ladder-like daises, the middle one of which Commodus would doubtless soon be required to ascend.

It was at the corners of this block that the youths had deposited their lamps, and the base of it being somewhat narrower than the top, the meal spread out above for our consumption was not therefore brightly illumined. A good thing in a way, I suppose, when you consider that the 'meal' was in fact composed of nothing other than a fifth blindfolded youth (blindfolded and, I need hardly add, tightly bound), from the looks of him every bit alive as the other four, if, understandably, a shade more subdued.

I moved closer still, just to check that Commodus's predictions about the mode of sacrifice were correct, and noted with relief that they were. The body of the victim was carefully covered, only head and feet protruding at either end, but it was abnormally long and abnormally lumpy. And this was exactly what Commodus had said to look out for – lumpiness. 'They will use a dwarf for the bottom part,' he said, 'of that there is no doubt. But not only will they have to conceal him, they will have to include some kind of divisory partition so that the knife falls cleanly and safely, and they will also have to make some sort of provision for the blood. A pig's bladder, I would imagine, full of the stuff, or else a leather flask.'

From where I stood, I could discern no actual traces of any of these things, but there was certainly room enough for them all under the ample folds of the covering. So in order to put my mind quite at rest I edged my way nonchalantly round to the other end of the altar block and took a good look at the feet. They were small, but broad and calloused, definitely not the feet of a child, not even of an urchin bred in the streets. I caught the Emperor's eye and nodded at him, signalling that he could proceed as arranged. I reckoned things would go off very well.

And so they did, just as we had foreseen, if not better. In the inevitable uproar which followed the actual unmasking of the trickery there were scuffles and exchanges of insults and blows, and a certain amount of crushing and trampling as people tried to reach the altar to lay their hands on those responsible, but I think I can safely say that the only blood to be spilt was that in the bladder. Which was there, under the folds of the blanket, precisely where Commodus had said it would be, and which he held up in feigned surprise for all to see, and then slit to great effect right over one of the priest's heads. Over one small point alone our knowledge of human nature failed us: we had banked on the child being the first to scream, whereas in fact it was the dwarf. But apart from this everything went off exactly to plan. Commodus played his part beautifully, but then his shyness never did bother him when he was acting a role; I had noticed this from the schoolroom. Impossible for anyone, even the other celebrants at his elbow, to question his good faith. I have never seen a face express such innocence, such fervour, such a touching desire to do the right thing, and then, when it came to getting his way over the execution, make such a smooth and credible transition to utter cussedness and foolishness.

He timed things very carefully. He waited until all was made ready, allowed himself to be robed and wreathed and decked out in his priestly paraphernalia, nodded brightly as he was given his final instructions, and then solemnly mounted the dais, flanked by the other two priests. It was not until the very last moment when the point of sacrifice was reached and the priest to his right placed a guiding hand on the hilt of the sword together with his own, that he began to show signs of slight imperial intractability.

And it was here that the fun began. Commodus shook the hand off, muttering something. The priest replaced it. Commodus shook it off again, and again the priest replaced it. This sequence was repeated several times in growing embarrassment on the priest's part, until the man's face suddenly cleared and he indicated to his colleague that he thought the Emperor wished to use his left hand. A little more shuffling and muttering, then the business was repeated with the other hand and the other priest.

The assembly was tense, but, I think for other reasons, the preliminary swordplay did not seem to interest them much. They began to sit up and take notice, though, when Commodus, his hand at last freed, started to wield the blade above his head with what was no doubt an unusual show of vigour for an officiant, and then brought it to rest, very menacingly, directly above the victim's head. I was sorry for the boy, who I could see had lost his air of spurious suffering and begun to sweat real sweat, but reckoned the fright would do him no harm in the long run, maybe even some good.

Quick as an eel, one of the priests intervened and shifted the sword to where it was meant to be. Just as quickly Commodus shifted it back. This series of movements too was repeated several times. Then the man leant earnestly towards Commodus, no doubt in a last attempt to remind him of the original directives and get him to abide by them.

Commodus listened, pouting and frowning. 'No,' he said loudly when the priest had finished speaking. 'I prefer to do it my way. The middle is not a noble place, it is not where a sacrificial victim should be felled. A victim should be felled either by a blow to the neck, or else . . .' and he stretched out his arm past the second officiant, nearly toppling him from his ladder, 'or else a severe maiming blow to the legs – whack, like this, and then back to the neck again!'

I seem to remember that we had prepared more stratagems in the event of unforeseen difficulties such as the victims being drugged and failing to move, or the priests, as a last resort, consenting to the sacrifice and then falling back on a substitute child for the resurrection scene. But no stratagems were necessary seeing that at this point the poor little threatened 'legs' rose of their own accord with a deafening howl, threw back the blanket and exposed the entire machinery of the trick, bladder of blood included, which, as I said, was the only liquid of its kind to be shed.

No human blood, therefore, no death, no violence, a minimum of suffering, and profanation, if anything, on the part of the cult's leaders – in such, believe it or not, consisted the iniquitous Mithraic Murder.

IN CORPORE VILI
(Or the furtive road to knowledge.)

I don't know about belief exactly but one thing is certain: the Senator's ears are mine now, and so is the mind that lies between them. (A little broader this space than at the start of our acquaintance, or do I imagine things?) If I were to interrupt my visits I think he would have to send for me in order to know the rest. The squid is said to be the most curious of living creatures and easy to catch on that account, but fortunately for me it seems that Cassius comes a close second. My account of the so-called 'Murder' has shocked him of course, quite as much as if it had involved a real killing, if not more so, but it has shocked him in a captivating way. I can tell this mainly by the lack of all articulate comment on his part when I finish speaking, but also by the slackness of his jaw muscles under my touch: the senatorial mouth is literally hanging open with surprise.

And the other atrocity stories? he asks when he has mastered his mandible again. The ones concerning the concubines, and the prisoners, and the elimination of a quarter of the members of the Senate? Do I have alternative explanations to offer for those as well? Were they too prompted by reasons of State and designed to further some mysterious overall policy – the nature of which, incidentally, despite my various allusions, he is still totally unable to grasp? He would be grateful if I would suspend my massage for the time being – it is not proving a help to his concentration today – and just go ahead and give him a clear answer.

In particular, he adds – not because these were anecdotes he ever intended to use in his History: they are far too coarse and far too unpleasant, but because they are so detailed and curious that he cannot imagine anyone inventing them either wholly or in part – in particular he would like to hear what I have to say about the extraordinary incidents of the Fat Man and the Bird and the Worms. He will refresh my memory for me in case I have forgotten.

The first story, as it was told to him by his father, relates that Commodus, following a cruel whim and with nothing better in mind than his own entertainment, once caused a prisoner – an unusually fat man but otherwise healthy – to be split open like a gourd in his presence in order to watch the entrails fall to the ground and to see how long they were. Delightful, no? It also mentions that prior to the cutting of the belly the unfortunate victim was made to stand on a pedestal, the better to display the descent of the bowels. And not only, but that a charcoal line was drawn on the stomach by Commodus himself so as to ensure that the incision was made in exactly the way he wanted. The second story goes that on another occasion for the same frivolous reason the Emperor caused yet another unlucky prisoner to be buried in sand to the neck with only his head protruding, ordered a cage containing a hungry starling to be placed over the head, and then sat and watched while the bird picked the man's skull clean. What is more, besides indicating the exact breed of bird, the second story gives the colour of the prisoner's hair – black flecked with grey, and goes on to state how the bird went for the grey hairs first before it set about devouring the black, mistaking them for worms. A wealth of minor details which, Cassius thinks I will admit, lends disgust to the anecdotes maybe, but also an unmistakable touch of authenticity.

Alas, I am afraid that the Senator is right in what he says. Like the bird, one could pick holes in certain aspects of the stories straight away, just by using common sense and asking a few pertinent questions. For instance, one could ask whether a man whose abdomen is split open while he is standing on a pedestal is not more likely to fall to the ground himself before his bowels do? Or one could ask how long it would take a single starling, no matter how hungry, to eat its way through a human head and whether it is probable in consequence that the Emperor would have drawn as much amusement as is alleged by sitting through the entire performance from beginning to end? Or again, one could question whether a bird in such a situation would have gone for the hairs in the first place at all – black *or* grey as may have been – and enquire whether it would not have preferred to begin its meal with the eyes – softer, surely, and more nutritious? I can think of at least ten more questions of the kind which could be usefully posed. But common sense is never a very effective weapon to use against credulity, and even with the holes in it I am afraid that the fabric of the stories would still hold firm. They are indeed, as Cassius says, so peculiar and circumstantial that nobody could have made them up.

And in fact nobody did. Or certainly not in the sense that an oyster makes up a pearl – by producing it in its stomach, that is, out of nothing save the rays of the moon. But somebody made it up all right in the sense of putting it together.

Out of what elements and in what completely unfaithful and misleading order, I shall now attempt to make clear. And not so much for Cassius's benefit this time (for whom I will gloss over the truth behind these stories as best I can and then pass quickly to something else) as for my own. I feel no regret and certainly I feel no shame for the deeds my pupils and I performed but, as I once heard a famous old actor remark when excusing himself to a jeering public for forgetting his lines, old age brings confusion; and such things being abominable in all men's eyes but our own, and my eyes having lately grown so poor, I feel I would just like to reassure myself a little that our actions were indeed noble and correct. Or, at the very least, that they were not ignoble and not incorrect.

At the time I was assailed by no doubts of the kind. I was quite simply overjoyed when Commodus suggested to me that he, Marcia and I resume our habit of working together as we had done in their schoolroom days. I felt honoured, and I felt touched, and on the practical plane the thought did not escape me that now we would have altogether more freedom and more scope for our affairs. The Head of the Roman Empire holds the world in his hands; there is scarcely a limit to what he can do once he has set his mind to it: if formerly we had had difficulty in obtaining prime material, I told myself happily that this would no longer be the case.

Of course, I fully realized that there was an element of – not defeat exactly, but, let us say, forlornness about the young Emperor's decision; I could see that he was returning to his childhood pursuit not out of enthusiasm so much as a desire to escape the pressures of his office for a moment and procure for himself a little distraction. But under the circumstances, and provided the distraction did not last too long to the detriment of his statecraft, I could see no harm in his doing just this. Because the circumstances, it will be remembered, in the earlier half of Commodus's reign, were truly miserable – enough to dishearten a dragon, let alone a sensitive young man in his twenties. There were two main reasons for this, I think. First, the legacy, which in Marcus's original intentions was to have been so proud and glittering, came to his heir too late for it to be either. This was no one's fault in particular, but everyone's in general: Marcus's for failing to die with his body; mine for failing to see that he was already dead inside it; Commodus's for seeing but failing to notify me in time; Faustina's for dying so early – for if she had stayed alive there is just a chance that Marcus might have remained so too; and Marcia's, on the contrary, for being so alive and for forging through her vitality a link with the world that was difficult for Marcus to sever. With so many people responsible, the delay was in a sense unavoidable, but the fact remains that the legacy came too late; and as a result the first years of his office had to be spent by Commodus, not introducing new policy, not in developing it or consolidating it, but in clearing away the ruins of the existent one so that he could make a proper start. The treasury was almost bankrupt; the coinage – gold apart – virtually worthless; the armies were sick and straggling and hungry and had to be recalled on pain of extinction; and the frontiers, unguarded of a sudden, had somehow to be made safe by other means. Thus, there was a mountain of dull, practical, administrative work to be done – unrewarding and unpopular as it was essential – before the young Emperor could turn his hand to anything else. To give a very simple illustration of his plight, chosen with Cassius in mind, it was as if a budding young author were to sit himself down at his desk to compose his long-dreamt masterpiece only to find that his materials are unserviceable and that first he must cut his own rushes for parchment, and net his own cuttlefish for his ink, and perhaps even re-carpenter his desk and stool while he is about it as well.

This was one reason for the Emperor's heavy heart. The second reason, antithetical to the first but dependent on it inasmuch as if Commodus hadn't been so taken up with other things he would have seen it on the horizon and stopped it in time, was that the conspiracy came too early. Which meant many things, but above all, that it was carried out by people too young and too inexperienced to know how these affairs are conducted. Faustina in her time hatched a plot against Marcus – or adhered to a plot against Marcus which comes to much the same thing – but she did her plotting elegantly and suavely and left room for doubt and room for manoeuvre, so that in the end, when the plot failed, all she had to do was to blush at her mistake and all Marcus had to do was to turn a blind eye, burn a few papers without reading them, and take his wife back in his arms again as if nothing had happened. This is the behaviour of mature and sensible people. Commodus's sister Lucilla, though, was neither mature nor sensible, nor did she know the rules of this complicated but at the same time widely practised game. Like her mother's, hers was a sorry little move, generated by fear and lack of confidence and a desperate and very understandable desire to be on the winning side, but unlike her mother's it was made messily and publicly, so that there could be no concealing things afterwards, no tears and kisses and recriminations and forgiveness, only punishment and death for those involved.

To choose for their attempt, as she and her husband Pompeianus did, the main entrance to the amphitheatre bustling with people, and for Pompeianus to spring out in full view brandishing a dagger and yelling 'Die, traitor, die!' at the top of his voice, was badly engineered to say the least.

What it must have cost Commodus in human terms to lose in the space of a day and at his own instruction – not a quarter of the Senate, Cassius's estimate is exaggerated, but certainly nearly all his closest associates and friends including wife, sister, brother-in-law and most of the members of his Privy Council, I do not like to imagine. He never spoke of it to me and I never cared to ask. However high the price, though, I think it must have cost him even more to keep people away at a spear's length as he was obliged to do so afterwards. For after the quashing of the conspiracy, those he could trust he could count, not on the fingers of one hand even, but on the leaves of one stalk of clover: *I* remained – elderly, critical, never easy to talk to; the faithful dogsbody Cleander remained – elderly, critical, impossible to talk to; and Marcia remained, who fortunately was none of these things. But that was all; beyond us there was no one.

It was in this atmosphere of loneliness and desertion, then, with the wounds of betrayal still fresh and the cries of the punished betrayers still ringing in the air, that Commodus's suggestion of resuming our studies was made. But although, as I said, I was aware of this fact, it didn't dampen my joy in the least. My pupils were coming back to me. I was thrilled; I was as excited as a child. And I set myself to preparing our work-chamber as if I were a bridegroom making ready for the arrival of a rich young pretty bride. Two brides, in fact.

With the Washer's assistance I found just the right spot: not the apologetic little cupboard of a room we had used before, but a large underground outhouse once used for the storage of ice-blocks but now deserted, connected to the undertaker's domain by a corridor unknown to anyone but himself and otherwise inaccessible. The place smelt nasty when he first opened it up for me and I had a few doubts about our being able to use it, but I lit fires of juniper twigs to dry it out, bored air-holes in the ceiling, and the smell soon disappeared. The connecting corridor continued in the other sense, running on under the slaughterhouse and annexe and into the bowels of the Palace itself, but the Washer said it was safer not to pursue it: the Palace undergrounds, he warned, were a world of their own where it was better not to venture. So I followed his advice and not the corridor, and on my visits always approached the room through the morgue, even if this meant a long detour, and advised Commodus and Marcia to do the same. (I now think, however, that perhaps they did not always heed my advice, and perhaps this is how the stories were bred: by someone following them to the room and catching a brief glimpse of what was taking place inside? I can think of no other way in which we could have been discovered. We did keep birds there at one time, I remember – quite a number of them, and in cages too, and kept worms to feed them on – and we did quite a lot of measuring intestines, using carbon, as always, to mark the incisions. An outstandingly fat human specimen, though, no, that I do not remember.)

When I had cleansed the room and made it wholesome again – working all by myself, I stress: no skivvies, no sweepers, no polishers, just the world's highest-paid physician down on his knees with his skirts rolled up, scrubbing with all his might – I furnished it. I provided lights and trundled in a barrel of oil to feed them. I brought in a work table, an instrument table, three desks, three couches, three wash-basins; I fashioned bookshelves and constructed an ingenious kind of hanging cupboard where we could keep refreshments without the rats getting at them, and another larger one in the same design for our samples. In short, I made a love-nest. For my cherished pupils, yes, of course, but also for the loved-one I have courted in vain all my life long: Knowledge.

How many hours Commodus, Marcia and I spent in this underground haven of ours I do not know, but I can make a rough calculation. We began our sessions, as I said, shortly after the quelling of Lucilla's conspiracy, and we continued them, fairly regularly, up to the beginning of my retirement. Close on six years, therefore, which at a rate of, say, two nights a month and two hours a night comes to a total of nearly three hundred hours.

Three hundred hours. Three *hundred* hours? Looking back on it they might as well have been three, so quickly did they pass. I cannot vouch for my pupils, who it sometimes seemed to me came more for the seclusion of the place than for the actual work we did there, but for myself I have never known such absorption, never known such happiness. Our results – such as we recorded, for we did not deem it wise to put all our findings in writing – perished in the fire of the Archives along with all the other records, and are thus lost to future generations of doctors who will no doubt have to sit like I did listening to their teachers dispute as to whether the substance which fills the veins is air or water or a mixture of both, or where food goes when it is swallowed and in what alchemic cavity of the body it is transformed into flesh and blood and bone and sinew. But even so, and even if my oral teaching were also to be lost eventually and my school disbanded, I cannot think that even a minute of our time was wasted. It is one thing to have, as we did in Commodus's and Marcia's schoolroom days, a monkey's head or half a pig on the table before you (since however deep you probe it is still, at the end of the day, monkeys and pigs that you are finding out about). It is one thing to have, as I did earlier when I worked with the gladiators, some poor mangled fighter whom it is your duty to put together rather than pull apart, and who anyway wriggles too much to be of any real use. It is one thing to have the stiff, mouldy remains of some hapless creature who has been fished with great trouble and expense, not to speak of delay, from the press of a common grave (for this was my only other resort). It is *quite* another thing, believe me, to have a fresh, integral specimen of manhood who in some cases – depending slightly on the Washer's commitments and the size of the tip he has received – has only just that moment stopped breathing.

The Socratic doctrine says that the first step towards knowledge is one of humility: one must take a step backwards, that is, and admit that one knows nothing; more, one must recognize the fact with the intellect, one must *know* that one knows nothing. And this is exactly what my first confrontation with a real good serviceable cadaver obliged me to do. I was at the time – and I say it without vanity, merely with precision – the world's most capable and most sought-after doctor, with decades of experience to my credit already, and thousands of successful cases behind me, and scores of students who fought one another almost to obtain admittance to my lessons; and yet, when finally faced with this complete and unspoiled example of the human machine laid open to me in all its complexity with the labyrinth of its myriad passages perusable at will, I was obliged to recognize that that was what I knew: nothing. Or as children say when they play knucklebones, dusky-nothing.

And it was from there, from the pit of dusky-nothing, that my two pupils and myself, slowly, but as I said, happily and absorbedly, began to make our ascent. Probing, cutting, delving; cataloguing, counting, recording; and learning, learning, learning.

The fact remains, though, that absorption and achievement are no guarantee that what is being done is morally right. Doubtless the murderer is interested in what he is doing to the exclusion of all else; doubtless he too feels – and quite correctly – that his action will leave its mark. I was brought up in a school which regards human remains as improper material for study. More, I was brought up in a school which regards *material* as improper for study. Matter, I was taught, contains no truths, reveals no secrets. Matter is dumb, matter is base, matter is jumbled and unlit and unleavened and devoid of meaning. It is the *mind*, the reasoning and ordering force of the mind, which is the fount and dwelling-place of knowledge. The ancient sages proceeded on this principle, and behold the magnificent edifice of their collective wisdom. Only Empedocles chose to dissent, insisting on lowering himself into the volcano in person to inspect its belly, and look what good it did him. The cord that held him was burnt and he was gobbled up by the volcano. Punished for his mistake in method; punished for his presumption. Just as in more recent times Plinius Secundus was punished in much the same way for much the same kind of transgression: choked to death by the ashes of Vesuvius when he tried to approach the scene of the eruption in a boat to observe it at close range.

Attention, though, warned my teachers, I was not to infer from this that volcanoes were spiteful (although it should not be excluded either, and the further one kept away from them, the better). The lesson to be learned was another: namely, that the world of the sense is mendacious and that those who address their questions to that quarter instead of relying on Reason receive lies in answer, or at best partial truths. And partial truths, in medicine as in everything else, are just not good enough. For a doctor it is not sufficient, not even particularly helpful, to find out what in fact takes place within the confines of the individual body; no, what the aspiring therapist should aim at discovering is what *must* take place, in *every* body, in accordance to the universal principles by which all things are governed. And this, only Reason, Divine, Omnipotent Reason is able to disclose.

Did we act wrongly then, my royal pupils and myself, by presuming to interrogate humble matter, humble flesh, the way we did? Did we indeed, despite our convictions and the importance of our findings, commit a crime? With some tiny pockets of perplexity still, but I would say no, we did not.

(Beware, rings in my ears the voice of the vacillating, lost Marcus, half-engulfed by the quagmire himself. Beware, Galen, of reckoning the welfare of men on a par with that of livestock, that is to follow a will-o'-the wisp which leads to a moral quagmire.

But I disregard the warning and count in my head – for my fingers are not enough for me – the lives that my furtively acquired knowledge has enabled me to save, the people I have benefited, the deaths and the suffering that I have forestalled. No, surely, I was right. We were right. On this as on other matters, we were right.)

QUALIS PATER, TALIS FILIUS
(The question of family resemblance.)

So far the Senator and I seem to have been working our way backwards through the points listed in the notes, in shrimp-hops, and this has fitted in with my plan very well: the more outrageous the charges are, the less truth they contain, and the easier they are to disprove.

I have, as intended, kept rather quiet about the precise nature of the Emperor's and my activities in our underground laboratory, and have fobbed off Cassius instead with a milder explanation of how the stories he mentions could have arisen – namely from Commodus's habit (formed in his schooldays and greatly encouraged by me) of drawing. The young Emperor never buried prisoners in sand, I explain, but he did often get them to sit for him without moving for long periods of time while he made likenesses of them. And he used charcoal for his drawing as most draughtsmen do. And he often copied birds and insects too. So this is probably how the rumours started.

Even this alternative version Cassius finds so deeply distasteful and strange that I pass over it quickly, drawing his attention to another rumour – that of the so-called 'Palace Brothel', and explaining to him how this notorious institution was in reality nothing more than a straightforward kind of hostel or boarding-school in which Commodus – like every other ruler before and since to my knowledge – lodged the sons and daughters of his provincial governors and other high-up but far-posted officials to act as pledges of their fathers' good behaviour.

Here I meet with more success. Cassius, for once, is utterly convinced by what I say (because Severus runs a similar establishment today and several of Cassius's young relatives are housed there), and utterly indignant at what he defines, spluttering into his towel, as 'a most vile attack on the citadel of history. What *would* the great

Thucydides have to say about it were he alive?' He seems quite willing now to shelve the matter of the tortures, and I will try to make sure it stays shelved. It is the first time I feel he is really sympathetic to my cause and cannot risk losing the advantage that this gives me. I do, I must admit, have a slight itch to go back and ask him what accusation lies behind the curious title, adjacent in the notes to the ones he has cited, of the 'Dwarves Smeared in Mustard', since I still cannot for the life of me imagine what real-life episode this corresponds to unless it be something to do with the hilarious joke-banquet which Commodus gave for his opponents in the Senate, outmanoeuvring the whole bunch of them in a single evening. But again, all things considered, it seems wiser to leave His Excellency's memory unjogged. For all I know his father Apronianus may have been present at the banquet and have consumed the risible fare with the other unfortunate guests (which, although not devilled dwarves, I am told did include such things as peppered chalk and cow-dung). Anyway, I have no doubt but that the story was as foolish and misinformed as the other two.

So far, then, swimming in this sea of absurdity, the shrimp's progress has been quite adequate to my needs. Now, however, coming as we are to more delicate matters which cannot be swept aside like the brothel in a mere sentence or two, I think it is time I changed tactics and instead of trying to explain to Cassius what Commodus was *not*, try to explain what he was, and what all the other personages concerned were too, behind their public masks which is evidently all Cassius was given to see of them during their lifetimes: namely, human beings like himself and myself.

The proposition being likely still to encounter a certain amount of resistance on my listener's part, who continues to think, as we have seen, in terms of monsters and saints and whores and she-bears, I try to arrive at it obliquely, by means of an example. I know, because I nearly fell headlong into it on my first visit, that in the centre of the main patio in the villa here, not far from where Cassius and I are now, stands one of those splendid old pools-cum-troughs-cum-cisterns all beautifully tiled in what I imagine to be the proper old-fashioned style in multi-coloured stones as small as lentils. When our daily session of treatment is over, therefore, I wrap my patient up in a towel and edge him tactfully towards this remarkable piece of masonry, asking if he would be so good as to describe it to me.

Certainly, says Cassius, with pleasure. It is indeed a very fine piece of work. His cousins from whom he rents the villa for his brief sojourns in the capital are no longer as rich as they used to be – luckily for him, or they probably would not have agreed to the present arrangement which suits him so very nicely – and have carried out no refurbishing in years. In the case of household commodities this is a pity: I will have noticed, for example, the lack of even so much as a decent coop for the chickens? (If I have noticed? I could hardly do otherwise. The Senator, when it is sunny, liking to take his therapy on a day-bed placed in the open, most of our conversations to date have been carried out in the midst of these creatures and to the constant accompaniment of their clucking.) But in the case of the cistern he thinks it is very fortunate, this quality of workmanship being hard to come by nowadays.

I ask for a description, do I? Well, let him see. It is like an ordinary pond, really, such as you might find in the countryside; and that, he supposes, is the marvel of it. It is oblong, not round or square, and the border is decorated with a motif of reeds and bulrushes in many shades of green, all twisted and interlocking and irregular – there is no repetition, not even of a single leaf. On the basin itself . . . unfortunately the water is rather dirty, so some of the shapes are a little hard to identify . . . but, yes, on the basin itself, again in a totally haphazard and irregular formation, there are pictures of all the things you would expect to find in a real pond: newts, frogs, fishes of all colours and sizes, lily-leaves, flies, weeds – the lot. There is even a dead fish with its flesh eaten away and half its backbone showing, now isn't that amazing? The best way to describe the whole, really, is simply to say that it is so lifelike that it makes you feel like stooping down with a net in your hand and trying to catch one of the fish – one of the live ones, that is – for your dinner.

I thank the Senator for his very graphic rendering, and say that the cistern sounds even finer than I had imagined it to be. 'Although nowadays, of course,' I added slyly, 'the fashion is more for stark, simple patterns in black and white.'

'Ah, yes,' says Cassius, not perceiving the trap and walking right into it, faster even than I had hoped. 'But black and white tiles, no matter how cleverly set, could never give you a result like this. With two contrasting tones alone you could never achieve the same richness, the same subtlety, the same . . .' He snaps his fingers, searching for the right word.

'The same fidelity to truth, Excellency?'

'Exactly. The same fidelity to truth.'

It takes only a step to pass from the craft of tiling to the craft of writing, and I make it rapidly. And yet, I say, with all his appreciation of subtlety, with all his very proper regard for the truth, when it comes to his own work His Excellency would appear to be content with two contrasting tones and with a very stark and simple pattern indeed, seeing that his proposed treatment of the lives of Marcus Aurelius and Commodus is nothing but a sustained and unvaried antithesis, all the white on one side, all the black on the other. Does he really think, after all that I have told him thus far, to be able to do justice in this way to two extremely complex individuals, bound to one another moreover by the unloosable tie of parentage? Is this how he intends in his own profession to achieve fidelity to the truth? The shadow, which is all I am granted to see of Cassius, makes a brusque movement: I think he is turning his back on the cistern. He makes no reply but bellows for a slave and tells the man to summon my assistant who is standing in the porch outside as he does every day, waiting to accompany me home. 'The doctor has finished,' he says, 'and the doctor may go.'

Just as I am about to leave, however, he appears to have second thoughts and he catches my arm and presses it, speaking very low so that my assistant cannot hear. *Apart* from the fact that the antithesis is a very stylish and efficacious figure, he mutters, apart from the further fact that history *needs* stylish figures, and that the historian, like the tailor, must cut and shape and fashion his material if he is to produce wares of any significance: people do *not* go to the tailor to be swathed from head to foot in a bale of wool, and likewise they do not turn to the historian to be regaled with a shapeless mass of information. Apart from all this, he is willing to grant that there may be something in what I say, but only if the two men of whom we speak *were* in fact father and son. 'Convince me of this, Galen,' he whispers in conclusion, 'and I will concede you the point; otherwise not. And remember,' the pressure on my arm increases, 'I am best convinced by doctors when they speak of medical matters, so I advise you on your next visit to make your argument as medical as you can.'

Our next conversation thus takes us right back to the opening item on Cassius's list – the conception, and as requested it is highly abstract and technical. No memories, no stories, just a disquisition on the niceties and ins and outs (very literally in this case) of human genesis in general. A medical parenthesis. This calls for patience on my part. Despite the Senator's recommendation, I would greatly prefer to give my argument on a more personal slant: I would like, that is, to point to the characters and tastes of the two people involved, and to canvass on the Empress's side the implausibility of her ever having chosen as a lover a man of low and brutal habits when she was fastidious to a fault in such matters, and on the Emperor's, the extreme unlikelihood of his having countenanced as a cure for his wife's infidelity that arcane and savage method that is the human blood-bath. But I remind myself in time that this – the validity of arguments based on character – is exactly what I am trying to establish, and keep to the strictly scientific approach as bidden.

I am also careful to limit myself to examining the four versions of conception as given by Cassius in his notes (there are in fact others, but it would be foolish to draw his attention to them), and I retain his order. The only change I make is to label the versions for convenience of discussion: 'Blame on the Stars', 'Partial Blame on the Gladiator', 'Total Blame on the Gladiator', and 'Blame on the Bath'.

BLAME ON THE STARS: I am able to dispose of this one quickly, thanks to Cassius's practical nature which, on this point at least, is more down to earth even than my own. I have mixed feelings about the heavenly bodies myself: on the one hand I can see (no longer, alas, but once I could) that they are there in the vault above us in considerable splendour, and that they send us light and night and fire and rain and many other gifts besides, welcome and unwelcome, and that it is therefore little short of cosmic insolence to deny that we are to some extent under their sway and in their keeping. But, on the other hand, particularly where my profession is concerned, I feel that they are small and remote and that if any healing is to be done then I had better ignore them and do it myself. (I except from this reasoning the moon, of course, which is larger and whose workings are manifest.)

In this dual, not to say shilly-shallying, frame of mind I have correspondingly prepared a complicated defence which consists in: (a) drawing a distinction between 'influences' and 'determinations', then (b) drawing a sub-distinction in the field of influences between 'formative' influence and 'generative' ones, then (c) crossing the sub-distinction with the concepts of negative and positive to yield the very fine sub-sub-distinctions of 'negative-formative' influences, 'positive-formative' and so forth, and finally (d) arguing that the role of the stars in conception – unlike that of semen (positive-generative), unlike that of blood (positive-formative), unlike that of the womb, even (which, since it plays no active part but is nevertheless necessary to conception, must be termed negative-generative), is limited to the exercising of a 'negative-formative' influence. The stars can shape, that is, and they can alter, but they can only shape and alter material that is already placed at their disposal, and that only in a containing or repressive manner.

From here the rest of the argument follows very simply: because if the stars cannot determine, and they cannot generate matter, then they obviously cannot be held responsible for any physical trait – defect or otherwise – which constitutes an *addition* to the work of Nature. Diminished stature, yes; cleft-palates, yes; twisted or stunted limbs, missing fingers, blindness, deafness, dumbness, yes, yes, yes; all these things can, and probably do in some measure, come down to us from the heavens; but not bulges and not humps and not excessive hairiness and not excrescences, nor growths nor extras of any kind or description. And since, in the case of Commodus, one at least of the deformities was indisputably of this second kind – so runs my argument – the responsibility for its presence must be placed on an altogether more terrestrial agency.

Despite its fiddliness I rather like the reasoning, since it takes hold of a weakness (and the deformities *are* a weakness, there is no getting round it), twists it about and turns it into a strength. However, as I said, I am not called upon to use it in any detail because no sooner do I begin setting up my first distinction than Cassius intervenes with a blithely commonsensical remark, reminiscent of the barracks, and says that he has always known that to beget a human child you need something a little more solid and robust than a star-beam, and that as far as he is concerned I can tranquilly pass to the next point. A trifle reluctantly, because the argument was elegant and merited an airing, but this I do forthwith.

PARTIAL BLAME ON THE GLADIATOR: One rather drastic way of facing up to this second allegation would be to deny the relevance of lateral paternity to human conception altogether. The argument is one I have heard used by a colleague with great effect in the settlement of a disputed inheritance, and runs briefly thus: that while in many species, most notably dogs and cattle, indiscriminate coupling on the part of the dam both before and after fecundation can, and usually does, seriously sully the purity of the strain, the same does not occur in humans for the very good reason that humans are not animals at all but are in a totally different category. See, if in any doubt, the exclusively human capacity to make laws, employ logic, cover the pudenda and cook food.

The reasoning is bold, and opens up some very interesting new facts on the question of adultery. (An already pregnant woman, for example, would no longer be doing her husband any particular disservice by coupling with as many men as she fancied. Would she be entitled to do this, therefore? And if not, why not?) However, I do not think it suitable for my purpose, and for three valid reasons: one, because I do not believe it myself – I think we are very special animals, but I think we are animals none the less; two, because no other really reputable doctor of my acquaintance believes it either; and three, because with the nonchalance with which he has just dismissed the other philosophically grounded point about the stars and their influence, I don't think Cassius will believe it either.

I leave the drastic option aside, therefore, allow that in principle mixed paternity among humans is a very real hazard which can all too easily occur, and go on to argue simply that in the case of Marcus Aurelius and Commodus it seems to be unlikely that it did – or not, anyway, to any appreciable extent – owing to the uncannily strong facial resemblance which existed between the two Emperors. Who, not only by myself but by all who set eyes on them, were judged to be alike as two poppy seeds.

And at this point, to support my case I extract from my bag two busts which I have brought along with me – one of Marcus and one of Commodus – and hand them to Cassius and bid him to take a good look.

This move causes a short interruption. Cassius sits up, almost wrenching the statues from my hands, and gives a gasp – so loud that I am prompted to grope out for the statues again to prevent him from dropping them. He is clucking excitedly, like one of the chickens. I think it must be shock, or offence at having an effigy of the 'Monster' foisted on him without warning, but I am wrong: it is awe. Mixed with cupidity.

Do I realize? Cassius asks when he has got his breath back. Do I realize what this bust of Commodus here is worth? Why, it must be one of the few of its kind still in existence. And the ban has been lifted. I could sell it on the open market; better still, to a dealer; I could get a small fortune for it. How foolish he was not to ignore the Edict and keep his own exemplar. How very, very foolish. His was marble, too, not terracotta like this one. Worth even more. Tch, tch, tch, tch, tch. He is so taken aback, and so cross with himself about his lack of foresight, that it is only with difficulty that I am able to resume my argument.

Given this quite extraordinary likeness between the two men, therefore, I conclude (and as I do so I retrieve the statues and put them firmly back in my bag – Cassius's intellectual honesty is beyond question, but with valuables I never like to trust a fellow Greek), the possibility that the gladiator, or anyone else for that matter, had a hand in the fashioning of Commodus in the quality of co-father, can fairly safely be excluded.

A hand? Cassius intervenes quickly, recovering some of his spirit. Well, say I, out of respect for the late Empress, let us call it a hand.

What cannot be excluded with the same certainty, however, is the negative effect caused by simple percussion. *If* Faustina's sexual misconduct during pregnancy was indeed as sustained and vigorous as alleged, then I feel bound to admit that damage to the foetuses could, in theory, have been caused in this way – particularly, as Cassius's own notes point out, to the one situated in the lower half of the womb. But only damage of a very limited nature, like a bruise or a mark on the skin; certainly nothing more serious than that. (Cassius demurs over this for a moment, but after a practical demonstration consisting in me prodding my finger energetically into the folds of his own well-covered stomach several times with no harm to show for it, he eventually agrees.)

TOTAL BLAME ON THE GLADIATOR: Unassailable on medical grounds, bastardy being bastardy, even for doctors, but untenable on the grounds mentioned above of physical resemblance. If it is unlikely that an outsider had a share in paternity, it is less likely still that he had a monopoly. I tell Cassius I think we can safely skip this point and pass to a discussion of the last, and he agrees – this time without demur.

BLAME ON THE BATH: Historically speaking this is of course the most far-fetched and ridiculous of all four theories and I intend to demonstrate this as soon as I get the chance. But from the scientific point of view it reveals itself extraordinarily difficult to deny. True, the mouth of the uterus appears to close itself almost entirely during the period of gestation, and although I counsel my pregnant patients to be careful about bathing, I do not think there is any real risk of water entering the womb in this way. But the case is very different when we come to liquids such as semen and blood. Here we have to take into account the scientific attraction which the womb exerts – and *must* exert if it is to conceive and bear fruit – on these two particular substances. We have already allowed the possibility of lateral or secondary paternity: i.e. of foreign semen being drawn into the womb both before and after fertilization proper has taken place. We must also allow, then, that the same may be true of blood, and admit in consequence that were a pregnant woman really and truly to be placed in a bath of this liquid for any appreciable length of time, it is not only possible but extremely likely. I would almost say inevitable, that a certain amount of the liquid would indeed penetrate the womb. (Although perhaps not via the normal wider channel, but by tiny, imperceptible one-way channels situated in the walls of the uterus itself.) With what effects to the foetus it is hard to say, but presumably several, and if the blood were bad, presumably negative.

The concession is minimal but it is all Cassius needs. He jumps up from the couch and claps his hands triumphantly, scattering the chickens. So there we are: he says. All that reasoning and yet I am unable to make my case waterproof. That is – and he laughs – bloodproof. He has always known that one of the four explanations of how the taints crept in was correct, and now, thanks to me, he can see which one it is: the bath, the purifying bath. Of course, of course. Now that *will* be of assistance to him when it comes to writing about it in his History. He is very grateful to me for clearing the matter up.

AB ABSURDO

(Arguing from the absurd.)

The bath filled with human blood. Very well then, I say to Cassius at the start of my next visit, kneeling down beside him with much creaking of joints and beginning to rub. (To get the most out of his sessions my patient is always stripped and ready when I arrive, and today I see he is even pre-greased, like a capon for the fire.) Very well then, if His Excellency insists, let us now turn our attention to the bath.

This is what horse trainers call 'giving your mount its head'. I had been thinking myself of using the delivery-chair as the piece of furniture with which to begin my flea's-eye inspection of the imperial household, the moment of birth notoriously being a very revealing one for all concerned: no masks, no pretences; not only the babies are naked at such times as these. Thus I thought it might be a good idea to give Cassius his first real glimpse of Faustina as she sat contracted on the seat with nothing beautiful about her at all except for her hair – loose for once and untormented by the crimping-iron, her perfect little feet, and her immeasurable courage. Very rich women have so few opportunities for showing courage; I, who had only taken up my appointment a month before, had not yet realized she possessed it. Equally, I had thought it might be instructive for him to see the Emperor Marcus Aurelius, as I saw him myself every half-hour or so when I took him my report of how the birth was progressing, in the guise of a tired, harassed man of forty with stooping shoulders and a twitch in his left eye, sitting alone in the small bare room that was his study, eating currants and making use of this rare moment of solitude during which nobody but myself dared approach him, by catching up on his light reading. And I had thought too of showing Commodus himself, just as he appeared as he fell through the aperture of the chair and into the midwife's hands: no deformed, sabre-toothed monster snicking off fingers to right and left, but a plain, rather undersized infant marked by no peculiarities other than an inguinal rupture – admittedly large and unsightly – an unusual amount of hair, and two little front teeth just protruding from the gums.

This is the way I was planning to introduce my characters to Cassius – via the delivery-chair. But the blood-bath, I suppose, will do equally well. Just so long as I am able to get him to realize not so much that this particular amenity did not exist, as why it did not exist, and why it never could have existed.

I think it is as well for me to take Faustina first. The story Cassius has come by states that she was 'persuaded' by the Palace Priests to have her lover slain and then to take a bath in his blood . . . etc., etc. The word 'persuaded' is the telling one in the context. Faustina, from what I was given to know of her – which through the years and through the ups and downs of our intensely chafing relationship was quite a lot – was never persuaded against her will to do anything by anybody. Not even by her husband whom she respected. Imagine by the priests, whom she did not.

Conceivably, her father, the former Emperor Antoninus Pius, may have had some sway over her, I do not know. But from the moment she came into her vast inheritance onwards she was quite simply and incontrovertibly the most powerful individual whose feet trod the earth. (Very pretty feet, as I said.) She was not spoilt and she was not arrogant and she was not capricious, all of which things she could so easily have become as a result, but she was entitled to have her own way and saw to it that she got it. I was not an admirer: things might have been easier between us if I had been, but I do not think I am being unfairly critical either when in summing up her character I say that the Lady Faustina, inside her soft, neat, elegant little body which kept its shape so beautifully through the rigours of all the confinements, was as resilient and unpliable as the tusk of an old bull elephant.

Her power was perhaps not generally recognized – outside the small, privileged circle, that is, where the terms of wills and marriage settlements and the boundaries of estates constitute a kind of pool of latent knowledge in which all members appear to be steeped from birth, but, by anyone who set foot in the precincts of the Palace itself, it could be felt immediately. It ran through the place like a current, churning, flowing, and creating as its main effect a – not hostile exactly, but nevertheless tense and vibrant division between all those who lived and worked there.

Even on the outskirts, in the forges and bakeries and laundries and all the various other services which surrounded the central complex, nestling like a clutch of ragged chicks around the sleek fat body of the hen, you could see that there was Marcus's business to be attended to and Faustina's business to be attended to, and Marcus's people and Faustina's people to see that this was done. Preferably first. Bread was required for the Emperor's table? It was on its way, but with a slight delay since the ovens were presently filled with a special order of olive-oil rolls for the Empress and her staff. The keeper of the Emperor's wardrobe had come for the linen-baskets? Very well, but let him wait a few minutes; an urgent commission from the Empress's dressers had to be completed first. This type of exchange could be heard on every hand. It was not that these serving people were disloyal to their Lord or did not know what was due to him, it was just that they knew even more keenly from whose purse came the money that paid for their food.

I fell under the blade of division myself, being obliged, almost on my very first visit to the Palace, to decide and openly declare whose side I was on. The pressure of the blade was gentle, mind you: no grilling, no interrogation, merely a series of glances and innuendos and carefully phrased questions on the Empress's part – 'I would be interested to hear your opinion on this point, Galen, because my husband always maintains . . . whereas I tend to think . . .' but it was steely strong. That I chose Marcus's camp (who, it must be admitted, complicated the division by nearly always campaigning hard on Faustina's side himself), was inevitable but in some ways unlucky. It followed that I treated the Emperor himself regularly, and Commodus too when circumstances brought him at last into our sector, but it meant that in the Empress's apartments where the nurseries lay I was generally unwelcome.

Except, that is, when things were either very easy or very difficult. Faustina turned to me for tooth-polish and for my famous blend of glue (a habit she passed on to Marcia, as we have seen, and as Cassius has seen to his delight), and she turned to me for miracles. For all matters lying in between she had her own team of medical advisors: a group of envious and incompetent practitioners of a school directly opposed to my own, who were the ones to make the miracles necessary in the first place while at the same time making them more often than not impossible.

Such being the extent, then, of the Empress's power, where not even her lord and husband was able to contrast it to save the lives of his own children except when they were in the jaws of death or past them, to speak of her being overridden on such an intimate matter as the sacrifice of a lover by a posse of old men whose posts depended, anyway, largely on her favour, is an absurdity. (This conclusion does not appeal much to Cassius who has romantic notions about imperial power, and he jibs a little before accepting it. He knows what heiresses are like all right, he says, his own money comes to him from his mother's side so he knows only too well. But an *Emperor*, surely, wouldn't he – shouldn't he – have more power over his wife than the general run of husbands? Not if his wife owns most of his empire, I reply. Not if she is his banker and guarantor and finances everything from his bedsocks to his battles, not then.)

Equally absurd, if not more so, is to imagine that a man of Marcus Aurelius's moral stature would ever have allowed a plan like the blood-bath to be discussed in his presence in the first place, let alone undertaken. I do not put it past the priests to come up with the idea: far more discreetly than is alleged, of course, but Faustina *was* undoubtedly unfaithful to her husband, and an immersion in the blood of the object of desire *is* still widely considered a good remedy for infidelity for those who can stomach and afford it. Nor do I exclude the possibility of these men having tried, covertly, hopping and flapping round the subject like a gaggle of cranes, to put the idea before Marcus himself. But what I do exclude, and absolutely, is the possibility of his having taken the advice or even, once he saw what it consisted in, so much as listened to it.

How can I assert this with such authority? Well, let me see. Cassius has said that a mere doctor like myself cannot know the heart of an Emperor, only his skin, and there is a certain amount of justice in this. It is true that Marcus was a shy, aloof and fastidious man, and that he opened only very small compartments of himself to other people, and always to different people; so that while I, for instance, was granted an insight into his views about medicine and science and (as time went by our friendship deepened) philosophy and statecraft, and while his old tutor Fronto was allowed to share his opinions on art and literature, and his philosopher friend Rusticus his moral dilemmas, and Faustina his sentiments regarding the family and his money worries, and poor little Marcia ultimately his nightmares, to none of us was it given to look into all the cupboards simultaneously and make acquaintance with the whole man. It is true also that he was a great aristocrat and I was not, and that therefore we were, in theory at least, distanced from one another by our upbringing and experience of the world. (A senator like himself on Cassius's reckoning coming far, far closer, as he points out to me here with pride.)

What Cassius does not realize, however, in connection with this last point, is that Marcus had, by means of his moral striving, achieved a position where hierarchical measurements could no longer be taken, no longer be applied. If we picture to ourselves for a moment the State as forming, say, a cone or pyramid or an ant-hill, with the slaves and the menials, many and compressed, at the base, shopkeepers and businessmen in the middle, and landowners and senators at the top (and I rather like the simile, incidentally: I can see all sorts of extensions to it; can see ruthless little ants climbing up the sides, weak little ants sliding down, others stationary and clinging on to their position for dear life) – then it is clear that Marcus occupied the highest and loneliest point of all. But the thing to understand is that he occupied it, not weightily, statically like Severus does now, crushing those beneath him like a killer-sow her piglets, but lightly and feelingly. He was, so to speak, an ant with wings, outside the heap altogether, able to soar off the top and dip down to visit all the strata from the highest level to the lowest and to see what was going on there and to appreciate, if not actually share, the plight of those stacked in the various levels. (Hence his long-standing desire to do away with the entire pile: no pile, no pressure; no pressure, no pain.)

It had cost him much, this unenviable freedom of his: wings of that kind do not grow without trouble and sacrifice. He had lost, for example, the knack of making those intimate and warm friendships for which a certain dose of complicity is required; he had lost the common touch – if ever he had had it – and he had lost the ability not to lighten people's loads, because that was what he was constantly engaged in doing in a hundred practical and concrete ways, but to give the impression that he was lightening them. Supplicants, even when successful, generally came away from the imperial presence looking as if they had received a beating instead of a favour.

But these were trimmings, and the core of the man, to those like myself who knew how to reach it, was generous and considerate almost to a fault. I was his subject, his hireling, his servant and quite a lowly one at that, but within these limits I was treated by him at most times as an equal and at some times, when my knowledge warranted it, as a superior; never, never as an inferior. I honour myself therefore, because the honour was bestowed on me by Marcus himself, that besides or despite being his doctor I was also his friend. For so long as he remained capable of friendship.

This I think disposes of half of Cassius's objection. The other half is disposed of by the existence of Marcus's Journals. Extraordinary text which Cassius hardly likes to speak of, so deeply does it trouble him, but which speak of I must, so great is its importance in so far as my knowledge of the writer is concerned. Marcus did not perhaps open up all the innermost recesses of his heart to me or to anyone else when alive, but he opened them up to himself – with a relentlessness that no one before has ever used, and no one is likely to use again. And now that he is dead, there they are, all the secret little closets, exposed, open, their doors hanging wide, to be visited and rummaged through by anyone who feels so inclined. Some find beauty in the result, some, like Cassius, only pain and embarrassment, but literary qualities aside, all find information.

I do not, mind you, hold that the Journals provide a complete map to their author's soul. How could they when the writer was so incomplete himself when he composed them? But I do think that they provide a complementary one. Particularly to those like myself who already possess several other fragments. To put it very simply, my claim is this: that what I did not know of the live Marcus, which I am the first to admit was a considerable amount, I subsequently learned, via the Journals, from the dead one so that I now know him as well as, if not better than, any other person who was privileged to come into contact with him.

And contact was indeed a privilege. I am not, of course, speaking of the last terrible months when his body lingered on among us like an empty shell from which the life-giving principle has long since escaped, but of the time when he was himself, integral and unravaged.

The terminology of Cassius's notes is stilted perhaps, but otherwise I have no quarrel with the phrase 'the closest approximation to perfection that the race of mankind has ever expressed'. As I just said, traits such as warmth and comradeship and sparkle had been paid out like tolls at various places along the way, but the mature and complete Marcus, such as he was when he called me to his Court and such as he remained for the next sixteen or so years until the eve of his decay, truly came closer than anyone else I can name to being a perfect man. Which as I understand it means being both great and small at the same time, and small because great, and great because small. Having faults, that is, and recognizing them and fighting constantly against them. Overcoming these faults and never telling yourself that you have won. Being severe with the self and not with others. Treating your soul as an athlete treats his body but never pausing to admire the result. It means all sorts of things, few of which I have ever practised myself but which none the less I am able to grasp and appreciate. Marcus was clever – almost, I would say, as clever as I am – but unlike me he did not prize his cleverness or cultivate it at the expense of his other qualities. He was compassionate: in the region of his head rather than his heart maybe, but the sufferings of others touched him and he did his best to alleviate them. He was patient, he was tolerant, he was brave. And though slow and lazy by constitution he drove himself like a carter would a hired donkey with no regard for anything save performance. Complaisance was unknown to him: the reason may simply have been that he scrutinized them less mercilessly, but I truly think that certain people, amongst whom his wife who didn't in the least deserve it, he actually valued from the point of view of their characters a good deal higher than himself.

What more can I say? Very little. My regard is perhaps best summed up by the fact that whenever – as I often did and still do – I lost my patience with the human race and found everyone surrounding me foolish and corrupt and contemptible, I would remind myself of his existence and say to myself, 'Yes, that is so maybe, but then there is Marcus.' Coming from one as intransigent as me, it is not a bad recommendation.

Men act out of character, of course they do. I had a little mouse of a bondman once, greatly teased by his fellows for his meekness, whom we later discovered (much to the consternation of those who had teased him) to have killed no less than eighteen men by severing their windpipes with his teeth. And I had a housekeeper, a most modest and retiring woman with cropped hair and downcast eyes, accustomed to treating all males, myself included, as if they were rabid dogs, who, in her fifty-second year suddenly appeared one day in the garden, painted and bejewelled but otherwise naked as a worm, and began to dance a frenzied dance there, under the rain. But there are limits to such deviations, and even were someone to convince me that for some reason or other the Empress had agreed to undergo the cure of the blood-bath, and even were I to be shown the vessel she sat in with the marks still on it and the order of execution signed in the Emperor's own hand, I would never believe that Marcus Aurelius Antoninus, integral and in charge of his life as he was then, had any part whatsoever in the perpetration of so base and cowardly an act. I would sooner believe that snow is hot or that the sun is cold, or that a hippopotamus launched from a seven-storey building would travel upwards.

SIMILIA SIMILIBUS CURANTUR

(The homeopath's maxim: Cure the disease with
a dose of the disease itself.)

Having, I trust, emptied the bath of whatever argumentative
powers it may have contained in Cassius's eyes, I feel ready
now to pass to the more real set of charges relating to Commodus's
infancy.

Not so Cassius, I fear. At our next appointment I find my patient
inside on account of the rain, not stripped on his couch and waiting,
but fully dressed and busy trying to instruct a team of slaves how to
scrape the oil-fume marks from the walls without making any noise.
When I put forward the new topic of discussion he merely shrugs and
says crossly that unless he can get these muleheads of domestics to
work quietly we won't be able to discuss anything.

Anxious to get on with my story – because I have heard the Senator
is up for a new posting shortly, and there is much still to tell – I offer a
few helpful suggestions, such as the use of soap and sponge, or leather
strops, or wads of ram's wool soaked in vinegar, but Cassius dismisses
them all as too expensive: the dirt may be his, he says, but the house
isn't. So despite all his efforts to mute it, the concert of scratching
blades and brushes continues. In his search for peace, His tight-fisted
Excellency finally orders the couch to be moved from room to room
until he and I find ourselves in a quiet but very pungent store-cupboard
filled with apples.

Here, in this none-too-convenient setting, once we have got
ourselves settled and I have adjusted my nose to the smell (which I
don't know why but is one of the few I detest), I return to the subject
of Commodus's alleged childhood crimes and begin to organize my
defence.

Is it really necessary, though, for me to do this? I enquire before I
start. For me to defend a child, I mean – any child, no matter what its
rank – against the accusations of whistling and dancing and moulding

clay pots? Because these, so far as I can see, are all that the crimes for the period consist in.

Cassius, traditional in such matters, says firmly that he thinks it is, and with this he immediately puts me in a certain amount of difficulty. Because owing to the thorny relations which existed from the start between the Empress and myself, I unfortunately did not see nearly as much of the imperial children when they were little as I would have liked – or as good sense would have counselled. Nor can I pretend otherwise.

After the birth of the twins, when I set the seal on the discord by persuading Marcus to take one of his rare stands and utterly forbid the recision of Commodus's rupture which her rival team of doctors were so intent on performing, I was given to understand by the Lady Faustina that I had forfeited my post so far as she was concerned.

My status as official Court Physician remained, of course, and gave me certain rights: I was entitled (in fact I think I was *obliged*, whatever anybody's feelings may have been) to preside over all the Empress's future confinements unless otherwise prevented. I was likewise entitled to attend all deathbeds and all cases of the three great scourges – leprosy, dropsy, and plague – occurring among any of the close members of the family, male or female, again whether I was welcome or not. And strictly as regards the male children and irrespective of their state of health, I was also entitled to carry out a twice-yearly examination: on their birthdays and on the Emperor's birthday. Which in this case, Commodus and Fulvus being the only live sons so far and sharing a birthday, meant that I could see them in summer and in spring. The dates being close, I might possibly, had I insisted, been able to obtain winter access as well, but while the boys' health remained good their father did not seem to think it worth the fuss, and when I raised the matter with him he quickly let it drop.

This was my official position, which, had it been rigorously required of me to keep, would have meant that apart from the seasonal check-ups (which took place in their father's quarters anyway) I would have crossed the threshold of the nurseries in these early years of Commodus's childhood only four times in all: for two births, (one a twin birth, his own) and two deaths.

My actual position, however, was more flexible. For one thing the Empress's attitude towards me, as I have already said, was not always one of hostility but tended to vary, waxing and waning like the moon (a body which in fact occupied a prominent place in her astral birth-chart). And for another, her way of showing hostility was not always in banishment but sometimes, quite the opposite, in issuing summons after summons to me on a series of trivial matters, such as requests for yet more glue – this time for broken toys – or pomade, or ointment for Nurse's bunions. Thus there were periods, during the nine long years in which Commodus remained under his mother's tutelage, in which I was admitted to the Empress's apartments quite frequently.

I enjoyed, for instance, a moment of high favour when, the year after the birth of the twins, a third son, Verus, was born to the imperial couple, thanks to my handling of the delivery. (And I think in particular thanks to my presence of mind in removing from the midwife's clutches a pair of what looked to be fire-irons and turning the baby into the correct position for expulsion with my fingers instead.) I enjoyed, or suffered, a long stretch of disgrace soon afterwards on account of a profound disagreement between Faustina and myself over what a nursing mother should and should not eat: garlic, I think, was chiefly what it hinged on. The year after this I was briefly back among the stars again for a resounding victory over the croup; and then, bump, I was down in the stables once more for daring to suggest that the correct way to combat the invasion of parasites which followed the disease was for all those affected, nursery staff included, to shave their heads. (The proviso, naturally, did not refer to the Empress herself, but even so for some reason or other it angered her badly.) And finally, although I drew no satisfaction from being so, I was up again, this time for many months, when it came to poor little Fulvus's death at the hands of the bunglers.

On a rough estimate then, I suppose I would have seen Commodus in the course of his early childhood on, say, thirty-odd different occasions, maybe fewer. Not much, spread over almost a decade. And still less when you consider that my close attention was not directed towards him at all but, at Marcus's own request, towards the two other boys, first Fulvus, and then when Fulvus was no more, the adored Verus. All the same I think I saw enough to be able to reassure Cassius as to Commodus's fundamental soundness of mind and body. Barring, that is, the evident minor and not-so-minor defects.

This I now attempt to do. But no sooner have I opened my defence than I am filled with a feeling of great unease, bordering almost on sadness, and have to pause for a moment to discover what it is that is bothering me.

At first I think it must be nostalgia for a time in which I too was young – or young at any rate compared to what I am today. But I soon realize that it is not this, but the fact that I have made the same defence before, in almost the very same words, to no other person than Marcus himself. And with my memory's fondness for retaining the black spots, I immediately remember where and when and why I made it, and all the attendant details come back to me as clearly as if I had seen them yesterday. No; more clearly, because yesterday I did not have my eyes as I did then.

The bed – that is the first thing that I see. And after the bed, the dressing. I cannot show my rage because matters are bad enough for Marcus as they stand, but the contrast between the purity of the former and the foulness of the latter tells me everything I need to know about how treatment of this case has been carried out by the Empress's band of hired assassins who go under the name of doctors. They have changed and rechanged the bed linen, they have set bowls of perfume everywhere, they have prinked and fussed and even bundled poor little Verus into a clean new shift for him to die in, with I hate to think what pain and misery on his part, but the bandage, no, that has not been changed in weeks. (Why was I not sent for earlier when I could have done something? The question hangs there in the air between Marcus and myself; it can never be asked. Fruitless to ask it anyway when we both of us know the answer.)

The next thing I see – for I am keeping my eyes down so as not to encounter Marcus's – is the tuft of golden hair protruding frm the bandage, shooting up bright and vital like a solitary little sprig of corn overlooked by the reapers, and Marcus's hand straying towards it and rubbing it between his fingers, time after after time. It is a gesture that will haunt me always, and which will come back to me forcefully when, in reading the Journals, I come across a phrase, otherwise mystifying, in which Marcus, speaking of things that to his mind contain great hidden beauty, lists among others the two curious examples of 'the ears of corn hanging down, and the lion's eyebrows'. Whether in fact he had this particular image in mind when he wrote the passage I cannot say for sure, but I know that when I read it myself it is what I see: that incongruous little patch of brightness in

95

its putrid setting, symbol of hope or despair, depending on how you look at it.

Marcus looks at it with despair. I have urged Cassius to peer behind the masks of his characters and observe the faces, but the face Marcus wears on this occasion *is* a mask: clay-coloured, rigid, the mouth a slit, the eyes two empty holes. Am I aware at this stage of the full extent of his loss? Naturally I am not: I have been told little as yet about the Project and nothing at all about the Vision that inspires it; I see only that the Emperor has lost another son. Nevertheless, it is clear to me that there is something that wounds him in this death that goes beyond the boundaries of personal bereavement. And those boundaries in this particular case are set very wide indeed.

With Verus, Marcus has lost not only the second of his three sons, but his favourite. He is fast approaching fifty. His wife is younger and still at childbearing age, but she is no longer in childbearing humour. He is unlikely, therefore, to have others. The phrase which Cassius finds so expressive about the lion cub and the jackal would never have found place on the Emperor's lips: he loved his children, all of them, in a tender, physical – one might almost say un-Roman way. But even so, in some deep cavern of his mind – a cavern, perhaps, in which he himself does not care to look – a thought not dissimilar to this may indeed be lurking. Otherwise, why does he choose this of all moments, inappropriate and awkward for both of us, to ask my opinion on Commodus? Who is, after all, alive and well, and about whom there will be plenty of time for us to talk at some later date.

Reassurance, I think that is what it is; he needs reassurance. And not the doctor's reassurance – for it has already, if with tragic delay, been decreed that Commodus passes into *my* hands now for all his medical needs – but the architect's reassurance that the building of his dreams will still stand, even though the two main pillars on which he planned to found it have crumbled and he is left with nothing more reliable than a faulty half-pillar.

What can I say in answer? More or less what I now say to Cassius, of course: that the child is normal in every respect, save for – what can I call it? – a vivacious disposition bordering on the restless which makes it hard for him to attend to any abstract subject for any appreciable length of time.

Marcus's head is fortunately bowed again as I speak: he is still busy with the lock of hair. (He will continue to fondle it until the closing of the sarcophagus, nearly forfeiting a finger through his reluctance to remove his hand until the very last instant.) Are letters abstract, then, he wants to know? Is writing? Is spelling? Is a wax tablet an abstraction, and a stylus an idea in the mind? If not, why is it that the child cannot make headway with any of these things? Why is it that though his eyes are good enough for other tasks he does not even appear to *see* the letters that his tutor etches for him on his letter-board? Because he cannot read them, he cannot copy them, more often than not he cannot even say what they are. I say the boy is normal, and goodness knows how fervently he would like to believe me, but a nine-year-old who cannot so much as write his own name cannot surely be considered normal? Not in the accepted sense of the word?

I hesitate, trying to remember my last visit to the schoolroom. His understanding is normal, I reply, improvising a little, and so is his grasp of reality. He is clever at fashioning things and can knit as swiftly as a girl. What is told or shown to him he comprehends well enough, it is merely with his written lessons that he is backward. *And* with speech of course, he has a little trouble still over utterance. But this . . .

Marcus's fingers close over the lock of hair and his knuckles whiten. A little trouble? he says, interrupting me for what I think must be the first time in our nine-year acquaintance. A stammer which clogs the child to silence, which distorts his face into that of a clown when he tries to speak, which swells his cheeks and turns them purple and contorts the lips until all that comes out is air and spittle, and I call that a little trouble? The definition might pass if we were speaking of the son of an ordinary working man whose future task in life is to carry bricks or plant cabbages, but for the son of the Emperor, speechlessness coupled with almost total illiteracy is not 'a little trouble'; it is catastrophe, it is ruin.

However partial my understanding of Marcus's intentions may be at this stage (and, as I said, it is still fairly partial, because he is still cagey about revealing his plans to me), I begin to appreciate the size of the problem he is faced with. And as with all problems, once my attention has been drawn to it, my instinct is not to spend time berating myself or anyone else for not having seen it earlier, but to grab hold of it immediately, turn it about and look at it from every angle and see what can be done to solve it.

I explain to Marcus, therefore, because the truth of this is the first thing that strikes me when I begin to think closely of the matter, that

Commodus stutters worst of all when he is in his father's presence, suggesting a nervous element in the disorder which we may be able to eradicate.

The words are intended as comforting, but they do not, alas, have this effect. Marcus lets go the thread of hair, raises his head and stares at me with his terrible hollow eyes. 'A nervous element?' he says. 'Then you too fear that the child is unbalanced in some way? Tell me, is that what you mean, that you detect signs of . . . of . . .?' He cannot bring himself to utter the dreaded word and is unable to find another.

'Madness?' I reply: I always like to air things, even concepts. 'No, I see no signs of madness. Any more than I see signs' (because I know what the next anguished query is going to be) 'of cowardice. The child is nervous, unsettled in your presence, that is all. And this . . . I am not saying that it is, mind you, but this could, I think, be the reason, or one of the reasons, for the difficulty he encounters with his speech. You – ' I correct myself hastily: an ounce more of blame on Marcus's shoulders with the weight they are presently bearing and I think they would snap – 'I have not perhaps paid quite enough attention to the child in the past. Or certainly not in the light of present events. There have been reasons for this lack of attention, and valid ones, but now there are reasons for making up for it, and with all haste. If you allow me a free hand – in everything that concerns the child, I mean, not only his health, but everything, and if you at the same time prevent the interference of all other hands,' I pause, laying great stress on the 'other' so that there is no mistaking whose I am referring to: my victory today is bitter but incisive and I must follow it up while I can, 'then I think there is a chance of your having in Commodus, one day and perhaps not such a distant day either, a son you can be proud of. Or at least,' and I pause again here to cut the claim down a little: a therapist learns to be cautious in his promises, 'a son of whom you need not be ashamed.'

Marcus lowers his head again in what I take to be a token of assent, but is evidently not only that. His hand resumes its caressing movement on the tuft of hair which is already beginning to lose some of its lustre. 'The light of present events,' he says, 'the light of present events.' And then, after a long moment, in a voice just as sad, 'Very well Galen, go ahead, he is yours for what you can make of him.'

My grooming or taking-in-hand, one might even say under the circumstances my recovery, of Commodus began with no loss of time the day after his brother's funeral. The boy smiled at intervals during this brief ceremony (Marcus had insisted on a very swift and simple rite), and broke into a skip as he approached the bier with his farewell gifts, creating a bad impression on the other mourners, but I put this down myself to his excitement at the changes that were in store for him, not in any way to pleasure at his younger brother's death. He was only four when his twin brother Fulvus died, and yet I was told by the nurse that he missed him badly and often asked after him – where he had gone to, when he was coming back, and I am sure these were the sentiments he felt for Verus now. Only of course in the interim he had discovered the futility of asking questions or hoping for a return. It is conceivable that he may have been a little wounded sometimes by the great affection that Marcus bore – and *showed* that he bore – towards Verus, but resentful, no. I don't think Commodus even knew what resentment was. (Nor envy either for that matter, nor jealousy, for otherwise what ought he to have done at Marcus's funeral, I ask myself? Danced like a maenad?) Anyway, all this is to say that unlike the others present I saw nothing very terrible in the skipping and did not interpret it as a sign of evil temper. Though of course there were undeniable oddities.

I had, I repeat, never before turned the beam of my attention on the rather curious problems which affected this third, less favoured, son of Marcus, nor had I ever given much thought to educational matters in general.

Strange in a way, because the moment I began to examine them I found them utterly fascinating and absorbing. But then I suppose this would have held true of everything: even when I boiled glue for the Empress, I was wholly taken up by the problems of glue-boiling to the point where I dreamt of them at night – great cauldrons of hare and rabbit bones bubbling away inside my head as my sleeping self tried to decide which was the best sort of bone to use.

My first move, and one I always make even in the sickroom when I am faced with something I know very little about, was to observe. I had a couch brought into a corner of the room where Commodus studied with his tutor (I am an enemy, as I have said before, to sitting for long periods of time); I had a rush screen placed before the couch so that I myself was *not* observed, because I had already guessed quite correctly the child's increased awkwardness in the presence of his father and felt that my own might have a similar effect – until, that is, it grew more familiar; and from behind the screen I lay quietly and watched, for several weeks, the lessons in progress. It was not an encouraging spectacle, and, despite what I had said to his father about Commodus's normality, I began to share some of Marcus's forebodings.

The child was graceful, even pretty, he had his father's air of extreme gravity and thoughtfulness, and when he came into the schoolroom he would salute his teacher with a charming little formula (which I noticed seemed to trip off his tongue smoothly enough) and give a wry smile which made him look for an instant almost older than his years; but the moment he sat down at his writing-table and took up his position of study, these signs of civility would disappear and he would revert to an almost capricious state of babyhood, drumming his heels, staring about him vacantly, nibbling on his stylus, giggling, biting his nails on his one available hand, and doing anything and everything he could to while away the six-hour period without profit.

He was never discourteous, never rowdy, never flagrantly disobedient. He listened to what his tutor said and made efforts to carry out the simple tasks required of him – like forming a row of pothooks on his tablet, or drawing circles, or copying out a single short word. But after the first uncertain strokes you would see his attention straying – where, it was hard to say when the room was so bare – and his hand would become listless and his face turn obstinate and blank, and he would revert to his fidgeting. Sometimes even rocking himself backwards and forwards on his seat and carrying his thumb to his mouth as if he were a new-born infant. I could understand now why Marcus, even on those rare occasions when he was free to do so, did not care to attend these lessons himself.

The six hours over and his arm freed once more, the boy would then rise and salute his teacher much as he had done on entry – although with less assurance and holding his head a little lower, repeat the list of homework that he had been assigned for the next day (an empty gesture because he never to my knowledge did the work), and take his leave. What his face looked like when he reached the other side of the curtain I do not know, but I imagine brighter as I could hear the pace of his steps down the corridor, growing faster and faster and then breaking into a run.

The first week I lay in my hiding-place and watched this

disheartening spectacle repeat itself. The second week I lay and watched and made notes. The third I began to make recommendations. I did not speak yet to Pitholaus, the tutor, partly because I did not want his knowledge of the situation to influence me, partly because he was the subject of my first recommendation.

Do not misunderstand me, the man was kindly and patient and an experienced teacher, and I had no quarrel with the way he conducted his lessons. Nor did I really disagree much with his basic assumption that it was useless to introduce Commodus to higher subjects such as rhetoric, Greek and Latin, until he could speak properly and read and write: there are stages to be observed in all things, and, as the saying goes, a bird must grow feathers before it can fly. All the same, I thought it possible that just as there might be an element of shyness behind the problem of the stammer, so too behind the problem of learning there might be an element of boredom pure and simple, and I decided therefore that it might not be a bad idea to introduce a few new faces into the schoolroom. I had noticed that even the screen had acted as a stimulant for a while, until the child had been told that there was nothing and nobody behind it. So my first suggestion was that Pitholaus, who outside lesson hours appeared to have a very different and quite friendly relationship with his young pupil, taking walks with him and playing bowls and even, when no one else was present, helping with his knitting, be allowed to remain at his post in quality of general preceptor, but that three or four younger tutors be engaged to conduct the actual teaching.

My other recommendations, all of them more or less with the same end in mind, were as follows: (i) that irrespective of progress in the basic disciplines the curriculum be immediately broadened to include history and poetry and the reading of stories (this on the as yet unwarranted assumption that Commodus's feathers *were* there, somewhere, and only needed using); (ii) that the child no longer study alone but with a companion, and (iii) that this companion be of his own age and not – as had apparently been tried before with bad results – of his own ability; (iv) that he be put to work in a larger and better lighted room with, if possible, a low-set window or an open door which would permit him to see what was going on outside; (v) that the hours of study be reduced to five, with a short interval for stretching the legs at the start of each hour; and lastly (vi) that no more insistence be placed on his wearing the heavy sling-contraption which Pitholaus placed such faith in and which I could see Commodus chafed under like a blood-horse under the yoke, but that he be asked instead, as a point of honour, to refrain voluntarily from using the offending hand.

All fanciful innovations which flew in the face of common sense, said Pitholaus when informed of them. Guaranteed to produce exactly the opposite result to the one desired. I spoke of blood-horses, but it was clear that I knew nothing about them since I had apparently never heard of curbs and martingales and blinkers.

Unfortunately, to begin with it seemed that Pitholaus was right. I attended the new lessons regularly myself – openly this time, no screen to hide me – and was, I must admit, dismayed by what I had brought about. No suitable companion had yet been found to study with Commodus, so the changes I had urged were not yet complete, but already the adoption of my other suggestions had borne fruit. And a very questionable kind of fruit, turning what formerly had at least had the merit of being a controlled and quiet event into a kind of agitated pantomime. Commodus did not fidget any longer, he rollicked; he did not grudge his attention to his teachers, he withdrew it completely and bestowed it scornfully elsewhere. The window, paned at my insistence with the very finest and most transparent glass, proved especially noxious. I had thought it would brighten the boy's mood to have something other than the four bare walls of the schoolroom to look at now and again and put him in a keener frame of mind for learning, but he abused my trust by looking nowhere else during the entire lesson period. The new tutors might not have been there at all for the attention he paid them.

Pitholaus was radiant as well he might have been, seeing in my failure a vindication of his own methods. No doubt he reckoned things would now go back again to the way they were before. He quoted Plato at me mischievously: to each men his own trade, the cobbler to cobbling, the teacher to teaching, and – he did not say as much but the implication was clear – the interfering doctor back to his doctoring again.

But I am not a man to stop short at a single setback. In medicine I have noticed that a worsening of the disease often precedes the cure, and there is nothing more dangerous than turning back at this delicate stage and trying to interrupt or reverse treatment. Pussy-footed therapists who dither are the ones who generally do the worst damage of all. The new measures were not proving successful?

Very well then, I would think up more of them: I would double the dose.

Short of putting Commodus to study in a seat at the theatre, though, I did not really see how this increase of dosage could be achieved. The companion? Of course, but the choice had to be a careful one and was not a measure that could be introduced overnight. More subjects, more teachers, more air, more windows? All things considered, I thought it better to leave these things as they were. Fewer hours? Five were already ludicrous. What, then? What other changes could I introduce?

The inspiration – because that is what it turned out to be – pure, sheer felicitous wheeze, for which I can claim no merit – came to me suddenly. During one of the lesson times as a matter of fact. I would like to claim that I had been reflecting deeply on the theory of the Table of Opposites and had already, years before I was to make my great discovery, noticed that there was something shaky in its application to the human frame, but this was not so. I wasn't thinking of anything in particular. I was just rattled and exasperated by watching this child who in other contexts seemed intelligent enough, make a fool of himself, and make fools of five grown men while he was about it.

Not with any premeditation therefore, but merely acting on impulse and an angry one at that, I stalked over to the desk where Commodus was sitting, twisted his head round to face mine (the eyes were full of tears, I noticed, which took the edge off my anger at once, because I realized here might lie the reason for much of the window-gazing) and gave him a hard, level, student-freezing look to show him I was to be trifled with no longer. Then I took his left hand, which had been lying on the surface of the table all morning, twitching like a landed fish, opened it, placed the stylus in it – or rammed the stylus into it would be more exact – and told him curtly to go ahead and write like that if he was capable.

Gasps of disapproval from the three under-tutors, a gasp from the child as well, a cry, almost a shriek from Pitholaus, and then, in the silence that followed, the sound of the stylus on the tablet and the gradual appearance of the word for the day – Justice, I think it was – in quavering outline in the wax.

Again, it would have been nice to add a little gloss to things and say that the moment was miraculous, a turning-point, and that

Commodus as a student never looked back. But here too it would not be quite the truth. It was *a* turning-point, but there were others, leading us backwards and forwards in the critical weeks that followed. The hand lacked exercise and the writing was not good; the eyesight remained faulty and it was in fact almost a year before copying became anything like accurate; sometimes words would be written in reverse, sometimes they would be spelt without vowels, sometimes as many as three or four vowels would appear in a row; and with growing pleasure in books the stutter became temporarily much, much worse. (And this, incidentally, may have been where the story of the whistling was born: Commodus in this phase of relapse being able only to utter his words after he had let all the air out of his mouth by means of a long deliberate breath very like a whistle, and the tutors and myself having contravened so many rules by then that one more meant nothing to us, nobody intervened to correct this tendency, and we just let him blow.) Nevertheless, the moment was without doubt a watershed in its way. Hardly intending to, and therefore with very little merit, I had proved my most important point: namely that the boy had the capacity in him to become literate. And also the will.

Of course, had I known then the truly extraordinary fact about the crossover of nervous fibres running from head to body (fact which Commodus, Marcia and I were later to discover together in one of our evening sessions in our underground haven and which was to delight us all enormously), I would have had an easier task in persuading Pitholaus that although very definitely on the left track, we were at the same time very definitely on the right one. All I would have needed to say was that a man who uses his left hand is in reality using the right side of his head and vice-versa, so that there is, so to speak, compensation going on continuously in both compartments and nothing to choose between them.

But I did not have this knowledge, and had therefore to sustain a fierce and vigorous battle against all four teachers, and against Marcus himself in order for my experiment to continue. *And*, I will admit, against my own inclination as well. Thinking habits and conventions I like to question. Indeed, my entire argument with Cassius is grounded on this assumption, that received opinion is not always the correct one. But there are some things that seem to me to stand outside the realm of criticism, so deep are they ingrained in our awareness, and the Doctrine of Opposites was, and remains for me, one of these.

Duality, like and unlike, negative and positive, odd and even – it is impossible to deny that these contrasts form the very cornerstone of our world. For what thought could there be without assent and negation? What life without male and female? What time without day and night? What medicine, for that matter, without dry and humid, hot and cold? One or two minor items, most of them recent additions, could, I think, be quibbled over: sweet and sour, for example. I do not think these necessarily exhaustive of our taste range or even mutually exclusive; rough and smooth, perhaps, cat and dog certainly. But the fundamental core of the table seems to me unassailable, flat and solid as the earth itself. There is the left and there is the right. The left is the side of the moon and darkness, of odd numbers and the female principle and the curve and of all things that are shady and dubious and evil; the right is the side of the sun and daylight and manhood, and of all that is clear and even and good and straight.

Believing this, and knowing nothing of the fibres, what then could I say to Marcus to convince him that it was not only advisable but necessary for Commodus – his son and flesh of his flesh – to write with his left hand? Nothing, except that the ruse worked. I couldn't say why; I couldn't say whether it would in the long run be harmful to his nature; I couldn't say that I totally approved of the idea myself; I could only point to the child – transformed and happy, wielding the stylus more and more nimbly, scraping away faster and faster at his slate – and say, Look, my lord, here is your idiot son jotting down passages from Thucydides. Do you wish to see him continue, or should he go back to his drunken pothooks?

MATER SEMPER CERTA

(We always know who the mother is, goes the popular saying. But do we?)

Cassius has followed me with more than his usual attention over the business of the stutter and the other handicaps, making me go over all the details several times and even mimic them for him. Perhaps mistakenly, but once again as I did briefly when I revealed to him the truth behind the brothel stories, I feel a quickening of something like real sympathy on his part, of convergence with my unprivileged flea's eye view.

I do not delude myself, mind you, that the sympathy is deep or lasting, nor do I fancy that the senatorial spyglass, although it may have been set aside for a moment, is really any less purple and prejudice-encrusted than it was at the start. I have talked and talked and massaged and massaged for days now until my tongue is dry and my fingers as numb as a leper's, but I still cannot really tell to what avail in so far as the furtherance of my aim is concerned. Do all my words penetrate my listener's awareness or only some of them? And the ones that penetrate, do they find hospitality there, are they accorded belief? Or will they, like the oil I use for rubbing, be wiped off blithely at the end of it all on a handful of rags and be cast into the cousins' incommodious ullage-pit? We will have to see.

But anyway, permanent or not, destined to pit or to parchment, my words seem now to have won for themselves another inch or so of His Excellency's credence, and during our next session of treatment – which thankfully takes place in the open again, far from the oppressive apples – he returns to the theme, having evidently given it thought in the interval.

His memories of Commodus's inaugural speech to the Senate, he says, are a trifle hazy to be honest, nothing like as clear as those of the Hunt. Largely, he confesses, because at sixteen he was so taken up with the impression he was making himself on the assembly as to overlook the young Emperor's performance almost entirely. A toga is not easy to manage with style until you get used to it. But he admits that looking back on the occasion and bearing in mind what I have just told him, much of Commodus's awkwardness and the extremely poor quality of the speech itself might indeed have been due to the actual physical difficulty that the orator had in uttering his words. Cassius's own father Apronianus and the other senators of his group were bitterly scoffing and put it all down to stupidity, chattering loudly and pointedly throughout and yawning and scratching and taking little strolls round the floor, but now that I have drawn his attention to this aspect of the thing he seems to remember that, yes, the p's and the b's in particular did come out very unevenly, so much so that the speaker was sometimes obliged to stop altogether – presumably, if what I say is true, while he tried to find alternative terms which did not contain these consonants. Fact which does shed a rather redeeming light on the matter, he is bound to admit. A speech without p's and b's is perforce a somewhat limited and unsatisfactory affair.

My views on left-handedness he also finds intriguing – of its being a simple quirk in the constitution, that is, and bearing no moral stigma. He is charmed, too, by the simplicity of the remedy. Funnily enough he has close friends with a son in a similar plight to Commodus's and will suggest to them that they stop tormenting the poor little mite with straps and exercises and just let him be and follow his list and see what happens. Perhaps I will help him explain to the parents when the time comes; from my lips the advice would sound better and carry more conviction, not least because Cassius has forgotten most of the technical part himself already. Am I sure though, he goes on, that in Commodus's case the arm affected the temper in a positive way as well? That there were no more of the listless moods which I said used to come over the child like a black blight and no more rages either? Because if so, then what do I have to say about the famous incident of the Bath-water, which, by all accounts, took place when Commodus was twelve – i.e. three years *after* the cure was effected? Is it simply the date which is wrong, or do I here too intend to dispute the entire happening and to put forward some fanciful alternative in its stead? (Oh dear, baths and blood again; Cassius seems to have a fascination for them. So much for the removal of the spyglass. Not even a minute has elapsed and it is already firmly back in place.)

I take my time here before replying, because in fact the origin of this widely reported but just as widely inaccurate tale is not all that clear to me and never has been. Certainly in adult life, Commodus *was* rather particular about the temperature of his baths, and would often prefer to have them overheated and then wait before entering sooner than face a chilly one, but I cannot remember this preference manifesting itself in childhood. What is more, if it had, I feel that it would have been smartly suppressed, seeing that one of Marcus's first moves on assuming tardy control over his one remaining son's education was personally to instruct all members of the tutorial staff to watch out for any signs of fads or whims in the child and to stamp them out mercilessly like flames in a cornfield. Possibly, there may have been a slight rumpus at one point in this connection, rather like there was over the matter of the blankets. (Dispute for which I hold myself mainly responsible: despite Marcus's insistence, I just would *not* allow that endurance of the cold is a good thing and nourishing to a child's soul. It was and remains my unshakeable opinion that the less cold is suffered in youth, the better the adult frame will withstand it when put to the test. And the same goes for hunger, *and* thirst, *and* pain. Training is no doubt essential to virtue and much else besides, but it should never be confused with wear and tear. As I urged Marcus to reflect, gaining from him at last a grudging acceptance: will shoes last longer because you have walked in them a hundred miles? Will a pot because countless meals have been cooked in it?)

Possibly then, as I say, there may have been an initial protest in connection with his bath-water on Commodus's part. Of which, presumably to prevent me from intervening as I did over the blankets (and not *only* the blankets: I am afraid I am a great meddler when it comes to household matters) I was not informed. This much I am ready to grant. But that the protest degenerated, as the story relates, to the point of the child ordering the death of the Bath Master by having the man flayed alive and thrown into boiling water to the taunt, 'Let him understand what I mean by "hot" by feeling the heat on his own wretched flesh!' – this is simply nonsense, another of those grotesque inventions which Severus in his cunning has put about.

As too is the epilogue to the story, according to which in order to humour the tyrannical youngster without actually carrying out his gory request, his attendants were obliged to flay a goat and throw its body into the bath instead. Quite apart from the fact that Commodus on the strength of our anatomy lessons would hardly have fallen for such a clumsy ruse; quite apart from this, the indulgence of whims, even harmless ones like a hankering for nuts or a yen to play the flute, was, as I have just pointed out, almost the first item on Marcus's new and very long list of Things That Were On No Account To Be Done, on pain of ruining the child.

I explain all this to Cassius as best I can, and as patiently. He grunts in answer and pats his spine, to show me the spot I am to concentrate on today. Very well then, he says, let us leave aside the bath-water and the tantrums and the what-have-you for the time being. I may be right; like the whistling and the dancing, these may be minor matters compared to the rest and have their justifications. (Although he notices that I have not been very forthcoming about the dancing. Did Commodus really indulge in this activity? He did? And did we try to stop him? We did not? *I* did not? I thought it beneficial to my pupil for him to move his body in time to music? What a very extraordinary idea. Wilder, even, than all the others put together, and one you can be sure he will *not* recommend to his friends. He hopes I was at least careful about which types of music were chosen.)

Let us shelve these issues for the present then, Cassius goes on, and let us pass to the far graver and more terrible charges of incest and parricide. I may take first which ever I prefer, if of preference one can speak in such a connection. He is correct in thinking, is he not, that I still do not intend to deny either of them outright? Merely to fill in the details and make them easier for a historian like himself to digest? Well, then, off I go. Let him see how I propose to accomplish this last and most difficult feat. No cheating, though. No evading the issue (because don't think that he hasn't noticed me doing just that some while back over the matters of the tortures). No juggling with words. A 'brothel' may be transformed into a 'hostel' by shifting a few letters. (And who is to say, incidentally, that fornication and debauchery did not take place inside the latter institution as well? His nephews have some very queer stories to tell about what goes on in theirs.) Left-handedness can be switched to right-headedness, irreverence for one cult may be passed off as championship of another and so on, but incest and parricide are always incest and parricide, no matter how you view them or what you call them. (The Senator turns over here. Despite the cataracts he evidently wants to look me in the eyes as he says this.) To kill is to kill, to copulate is to copulate. A father is a father – at least this was so in Marcus Aurelius's case, as I have been at such pains to point out, and a sister is a sister. The truth, then – this is what he wants to hear from me – the truth and nothing but the truth, as pure and simple as I can make it.

The truth may sometimes be pure – in this instance I like to think it was. Innocent, anyway, if not pure. But it is seldom, if ever, simple. For a start, Marcia Aurelia's position in the imperial household was itself anything but simple – even before I stepped in and began tinkering with it. Marcus and Faustina had adopted her quite openly, as they did numerous other children whose relatives they wished to favour – bestowing the family name on them, paying for their education, giving them posts and dowries and generally setting them up in life. But in Marcia's case they had gone further than this, had used a stricter formula, tied ten times more money on her, and taken her into the bosom of the family as if she had been a child of their own.

The official explanation for this unusual step (unusual, you understand, in so far as the child was a girl; over a boy there would have been less comment) was that it was made on the Emperor's initiative to console his wife for the loss of their son Fulvus, Commodus's twin. Myself, I find this extremely unlikely and did so even then. Admittedly, the adoption took place soon afterwards, but at the time of Fulvus's death Faustina had no fewer than five children living: she had her three daughters, Lucilla, Cornificia, and Fadilla, and her two young sons, Commodus and Verus, and from my close knowledge of her maternal instincts and from the way she reacted when she learnt, shortly before leaving Rome, that she was pregnant yet again, I would say that these five (and a bit) were already more than enough for her. I emphatically do not see her going broody, that is, and needing to be plied with foster chicks.

And nor, I think, did anyone else. Thus, the most accepted counter-explanation for the new addition to the imperial nursery was that the little girl was in fact Marcus's natural daughter, born to him by some barbarian woman who had caught his fancy in the north. But this, in view of future events and without counting the eyes and the complexion, seems to me not only unlikely but impossible.

No, my own theory, running slap against the popular saying that the father is always dubious and the mother always certain, is another; namely that the Emperor and Empress adopted this particular child in this particular way because she was not Marcus's natural daughter, but Faustina's.

A curious notion? Perhaps it is. Nevertheless, having given fierce and constant thought to the matter at one point of my life for weeks on end, at risk of losing my reason, I believe it to be true. Everything points to it being so; everything fits. It accounts for the bonds, the proclivities, the cross-currents of affection; it accounts for the money; and it accounts – and is indeed the *only* thing that accounts – for the apparent brutality of Marcus's subsequent behaviour (unless, of course, the internal decay had already started by then, which in a way I would prefer to think it had).

Consider the facts: Marcia was born the year before the twins, in exactly the same month that the Empress herself gave birth – allegedly to a boy and allegedly stillborn. The dates, therefore, coincide. Marcia's acknowledged father (and also, I am sure, her real father, this there seems no reason to doubt) was the Empress's Chief-Procurator, a man who not only did all Faustina's business for her and managed her estates and settled her accounts, but who also – and it can be said quite tranquilly as neither of them ever made much of a secret about it when alive – provided her with more intimate types of service as well. Particularly, but not only, when Marcus was away. The Procurator's wife had no children of her own and was most probably barren. Certainly at the time of the child's birth she was already gravely ill. I have this on the authority of the doctor who treated her, who, in a private conversation, excluded to me absolutely the possibility of a pregnancy on her part: the poor woman's womb, he said, was packed tight with tumours, big and knobbly as cauliflowers, and nothing could have come out of it save trouble. Which punctually did.

What I think happened therefore is this, that when Marcia was born it was agreed by all three parties, Procurator, Empress, and the Procurator's ailing wife, that it was in the best interests of all concerned for the child to be transferred to her father's house immediately. To which end it was put about that the Empress had been delivered of a stillborn child, then the live child and wet nurse were smuggled out of the Palace precincts and a curtain was drawn over the episode designed to be left there.

The reasons of the childless couple are not hard to understand: they wanted the baby with them. Nor are Faustina's reasons: the Procurator being dark as a Syrian and having those extraordinarily distinctive eyes, she did not want the baby with her one bit. Thus it was clearly better this way all round. How they accomplished the transfer while maintaining the secrecy, how they bamboozled and/or corrupted my predecessor and the midwife and whoever else may have been present at the birth, I do not know, but money works miracles and big money works big miracles and I can only conclude that they did.

The arrangement presumably worked well, until the Procurator's wife died. Then, I would imagine for a string of reasons, chief of which that there was no serious reason *against* it any more, Faustina simply wanted her daughter back under her own care. Her explanations to Marcus were her affair. I assume (I *must* assume if I am to continue to revere his memory) that she told him very little, and did not confess the truth until literally her deathbed. When I would not be at all surprised if she did not also suggest to her husband the drastic but infallible remedy for undoing the muddle which her silence had caused. And which he all too readily adopted.

Again, this is only an assumption, based more than anything else on the timing of Marcus's decisions, but it was given a kind of oblique confirmation by Marcia herself when she confided to me, years later, that the only reason why she accepted Marcus's proposal, otherwise so repugnant to her, was that Faustina, in a last interview shortly before her death, had urged her to do so if ever the occasion should arise. And she repeated to me the Empress's words, drawl and all, 'I would so much *rather* it were you, my precious, you understand, and not some greedy, ambitious outsider whom we none of us know. Oh, I realize he is old and tricky and that it would be hard for you when you have always looked upon him as a father. But if it comes to it, sweetest, do it for me, I beg of you, do it for me.'

If this hunch of mine about Marcia's parentage is correct – and it is, I stress, *only* a hunch, although in my own mind it amounts almost to a certainty – then the charge of incest has unfortunately more than a little substance to it. True, the charge is usually aimed in the wrong direction: like Cassius, people generally cite Lucilla as the sister concerned (why, I cannot think as she was by far the eldest and by far the plainest), or else, when Marcia is correctly identified, they limit themselves to accusing Commodus of revoking the deed of her adoption in ill faith so that he could have his way without infringing any law, moral or otherwise (act which in whatever faith was in reality performed by Marcus, not Commodus). But however wide the aim, nevertheless the target is hit, and the fact remains that unwittingly, even innocently perhaps, depending on how you are accustomed to view the concerns of Oedipus and Jocasta and the like whom I personally see as victims rather than offenders, Commodus fell in love and eventually married in all but name a woman who was forbiddenly closely related to him.

How much of all this I am in honesty bound to tell Cassius, when, as I say, some of it is still, even now, a matter of speculation to me, it is difficult to decide. The main culprit, for the incest as well as everything else, is of course sheer ill luck, but Cassius is not one of those who consider this factor to be random, impartial in its blows. Despite his sanguine attitude towards the stars, despite his mundane outlook and practical cast of mind, I am sure he will see it, or will in this particular case at least, as the visitation of Nemesis. And the misfortunes which followed, dogging the reign and making the Project itself so difficult to actuate – the ill-timed start, the ill-timed conspiracy, the plagues, the earthquakes, the failure of the grain harvest, the failure to produce an heir, even, perhaps, the spate of mysterious killings known as the 'Poisoned Needle Murders' when the capital trembled as a band of hired assassins roamed its streets culling victims as effortlessly as if they were daisies (I would give anything, incidentally, to know the poison that was used) – all these he will see as coming directly and consequentially in Nemesis's train. Punishment upon punishment raining down on the heads of the two aberrant lovers.

But this is clearly no more than empty superstition. In the case of the Conspiracy there may have been a slight connection, it is true, inasmuch as both Commodus's sister Lucilla and his wife Crispina may have had jealousy of Marcia among their motives in hatching their plot. In the case of the couple's subsequent barrenness there may be a link too, because the tie of consanguinity when it is too close does sometimes preclude conception, or else results in miscarriage – I have noticed this in mice. But apart from these two things, neither very certain, there is evidently no relation at all between incest and mishaps to follow. Not a casual one, not a moral one, and definitely not a retaliative one. Like cookery, logic and shame, retaliation is, I'm afraid, an exquisitely human affair and there is no point in our pretending otherwise.

AMOR ET DELICIÆ HUMANI GENERIS

(Love and delight of all mankind – and mine in particular.)

My final assessment of the incest, always assuming that my surmises about parentage are correct, which I have every reason to believe they are, is therefore that Commodus and Marcia committed this offence technically speaking, but without being in the least bit guilty or blameworthy of their action. It was, as I say, just another of the many misfortunes which struck them. Blind and fortuitous as all misfortunes are. The two lovers themselves were unaware of the blood-tie which bound them. *I* was unaware of the blood-tie which bound them – or was until it was too late for me to do anything about it. It was only half a blood-tie anyway and had its roots in the maternal side which is far less important from the physiological point of view. It did not disturb me when I recognized it and saw it knotting itself tighter and tighter before my very eyes (except for the problem of the childlessness which I have mentioned), and it does not disturb me now.

This being so, I hold myself totally justified in keeping my suspicions to myself even where they amount to certainties, and when I touch on the matter with Cassius in serving him with the straightforward thesis of adoption. I assure him, that is, that the rumours of incest are founded on nothing more solid than the fact that Commodus's concubine Marcia was – originally, before the bond was dissolved – his legally adopted sister, and with that I leave it. Quite enough for the busy little historian's ears. And after all, I have been asked to keep things simple. (This explanation of mine is met by another of the Senator's non-committal grunts, but I think it stems from drowsiness more than scepticism: my massage, perhaps the lack of drama in my story also, when he was most expecting it, has lulled him almost to the brink of sleep. I wait a moment before rousing him, because I have a little thinking still to do.)

In the privacy of my own mind I know only too well, of course, that the question of blame is more complex, and that alongside plain Misfortune there are two other agencies – both of them human and neither of them blind at the time – who must and do bear their share of it for what happened.

The first of these is Faustina. I do not go so far as to blame her for Marcia's actual birth – the girl's existence has given me altogether too much happiness for me to wish it undone – but I blame her: one, for keeping her silence about it for so long, and two, a trifle contradictorily perhaps, once she had decided to keep it, for not keeping it longer.

Neither course would have been easy, I grant, but I think her sweet Ladyship should have taken one of them and stuck to it. And then there were times, with regard to the first option anyway, when it would have been easier than others. For instance, the day I announced to her that with Marcus's approval I had chosen Marcia as permanent study-companion to Commodus and needed only her comment to finalize the matter – why did she not speak then? It would have cost so little effort. We were alone together, as I remember, in a rare moment of intimacy, in her dressing-room. I had designed for her a new type of mirror: an ebony tray filled with water which had the sole defect of being flat and hence rather inconvenient – for hair-styling in particular, and we were trying to think of how we could give a slant to it without spilling the water. A few words in my ear would have been sufficient. Faustina need have said nothing to Marcus and very little to me; she needn't even have looked me in the face if she didn't want to, she could have told her secret to my reflection. 'No, Galen,' was all she need have said, 'not Marcia. Commodus and Marcia should not be thrown too much in one another's company at this stage of their lives, and for the following very good reason . . .' and then given me it.

Why didn't she do this, then, when the moment was so suitable? Why instead did she raise her beautiful eyes to mine (tinged with reluctance, yes, but then her eyes were always tinged with reluctance when they left the mirror) and say that although she was sorry to part with Marcia and would miss her company most sorely, she thoroughly approved my choice?

The reasons I think are various. Probably Faustina didn't trust me. Probably she didn't want to give me any more leverage over her than I already had. Probably too she genuinely undervalued the danger that the situation involved, reckoning, much as Marcus did and much as I did myself until the facts forced me to see otherwise, that Commodus was nine and backward, Marcia nearly eleven and forward, that they had been raised together virtually from infancy without either of them showing particular interest in the other to date, and that the chances of them suddenly developing a great reciprocal passion were consequently very slight. Probably also, to do her justice, she determined, passion or no passion, to keep a watchful eye on the pair of them from now on just in case, and doubtless would have done so had she been able. (And to do her even further justice, and in case you think it strange that a mother should be so blind to her son's charms when it is nearly always the opposite with mothers – how do the southerners put it? Every little cockroach is a beauty in his mother's eyes – just in case you think this, let me remind you that although later Commodus was to be tall and blond and graceful, and to have his father's head set on an athlete's body, and his father's poise with none of his father's stiffness, and his mother's way with people with none of his mother's hauteur, and all sorts of other attractions besides not least the fact that he was scarcely aware of possessing them; at present this was not the case and he was just about as seductive as a tadpole.)

Most of all of these things must, I think, have run through the Empress's mind as she looked at me gravely with her fine cornelian eyes across the tray of water and gave me her consent. But what also ran through it, and far more murkily, was a current of family pride, not to say clannishness, not to say exclusiveness, so strong that I incline to think that my suggestion, regardless of its dangers, may actually have come to her as a relief. Again, I am only guessing and my guesses concerning Faustina are never very sympathetic, but I suspect that what may really have held her to silence on this occasion was not mistrust or embarrassment so much as the simple consideration that if a second pupil was to be called in to witness her son's humiliating struggles with Greek and Latin grammar, then he or she had best be a member of the family and a close one at that. Shortcomings, like riches for that matter, were things it was wiser to keep strictly within the bounds of the family circle.

In a word, then, what I chiefly blame Faustina for is her snobbery. Aggravated in this case as in others by her deplorable tendency to use

Marcia, unthinkingly, automatically, as if she were not an independent person but some kind of convenient extension of herself like a hand or a thumbnail.

My blame also goes to Faustina, in a rather contradictory fashion as I said, for lacking the coherence to abide by her decision to the end and for not allowing her tight-knit, all-in-the-family policy to reach its natural conclusion, however unnatural some may think it: namely her son and daughter openly wedded to one another, standing in the sunlight with the purple cloak of sovereignty covering their shoulders jointly. Bold, elegant, Pharaonic solution which, provided the cloak's incestuous undershift had remained hidden from view, would have saved a lot of headaches and a lot of heartaches all round.

On this point, however, I do not find it in me to come down on the Empress nearly as hard as on the others: coherence on one's deathbed is a luxury few can afford, and I do not doubt but that I too will waver when my moment comes, and call in the priests, and have myself laid out on the floor with all the candles and oak leaves and whatnots, and vomit out my soul. This, it seems, is the way we are all of us made: we like to lighten ourselves for the hypothetical journey that lies ahead, and Faustina was no exception.

With this I have more or less completed the list of the Empress's failings, which, when you consider that through no fault of her own she was to have no further control over either Marcia's or Commodus's upbringing for the next four-and-a-half years nor even so much as set eyes on them, were perhaps not so very grave after all. I come now to those of the second agency who is of course none other than myself – and which I thus prefer to call responsibilities, not failings. What was my part in the matter? How far am I to be counted answerable for the outcome? What, if anything, do I reproach myself for? What errors did I commit?

Instinctively I am tempted to say none, thereby betraying, per- haps, my only real error, but if so a very serious one: that of supreme and unquestioning confidence in myself and what I was about. I say happily that the Empress should have overridden my choice of study- companion to her son, and I am right, so she ought; but I sometimes wonder looking back on it whether this would have been possible, even for her. My championship of Marcia, once I had discovered her, was fiery and absolute. She was perfect for my needs, I wanted her and no one else, and I would have her and no one else. I claimed that in dark moments Marcus was the saviour of my opinion on mankind, well, if this is so then Marcia performed for me the same service as regards womankind. Gender which, thanks to my caustic, overbearing, unloving and unlovable mother, I tend as a rule to admire even less than its counterpart, making Marcia's achievement all the more remarkable.

Cassius's horrified description of the swaggering 'she-bear' who dominated the imperial box in the amphitheatre gives me no sense of outrage, it merely makes me smile. Marcia had a great fondness for honey and a trace of that much maligned animal's timidity, otherwise she had nothing of the bear about her at all. If I were to liken her to an animal I would choose the marmot, possibly the deer, and possibly a cross between the two with a sprinkling of the owl if this can be imagined. Given that her qualities included industry, inquisitiveness, liveliness, beauty, grace, strength, wisdom, loyalty, unassumingness, courage, and did not end with these, perhaps it would be simpler in a way for me to name those she had not, instead of those she had. (And certainly it would be less tiring for Cassius, who I have now pinched into wakefulness, and to whom I am of course relating this part of my story, carefully pruned of all references to incest, in a last-minute attempt to get him to revise his terrible opinion.) But this I do not like to do; I prefer to dwell on her a little. This must be because I miss her, even now. And how grateful I am, incidentally, to my friend the Washer for having the sense not to tell me what her body looked like at the end; I don't think I could have borne the knowledge, don't think I could have accommodated it inside my head without something breaking.

She was, yes, nearly eleven when I first saw her. First looked at her, that is. I had naturally seen her before on various occasions, formal and informal. I had seen her during processions, wedged into the ceremonial carriage with her sisters in their stiff little dresses which made them look like so many corn stacks; had caught sight of her once or twice trotting demurely in front of her nurses through the Palace grounds of winter mornings, head swathed, nose and ears stuffed with herbs against the cold in accordance with the bunglers' absurd regulations, and eyes – the Procurator's eyes – shining through the coverage; and had seen her too, perhaps more often than I would have liked, come to think of it, crouched on the nursery floor amidst dolls and skittles screaming her head off. A vigorous child. Apart from the eyes, though, which were fulminating, she had seemed to me unremarkable – a smallish, darkish girl verging on the swarthy whom circumstances had placed in a position above her merit, nothing more.

When I seriously began my search for a suitable fellow pupil for Commodus though, and proceeded to interview her, her sisters Fadilla and Cornificia and one or two other of the imperial wards with this end in mind, I was forced to alter my opinion sharply. Although how much I really saw then during that deep, yes, but rather brisk and selective examination, and how much is the fruit of my later knowledge of her character, I do not know. It always suits me to think I grasp everything at a glance; probably this is not so. But anyway, I saw enough to be able to discontinue my search on the spot and to send the other candidates relievedly back to their pursuits. None of them, I may add, not even Marcia, being very keen on winning the selection. Ah Marcia, Marcia, I have promised myself a bit of indulgence so I may as well take it and stay with her a moment longer. Nature is not often lavish with her gifts, not often generous even. Like a slave trainer she seems to be guided by the principle that to overdo, either in reward or punishment but especially reward, is to spoil. Thus you get clever people with ugly faces, and beautiful ones with no salt in their heads, and grossly overweight ones with the grace of dancers, and lissom ones who move like leaden crabs. And even from the most favoured, the most endowed, at least one or two important gifts are normally withheld (look at my poor Commodus) so as to redress to some extent the balance. There is even a fable about this, I think, although I am not sure I remember it correctly – something about a child's coming-of-age party to which all the animals have been invited, save through oversight the mouse, which then out of spite goes and gnaws a hole in the basket in which the guest's gifts are contained so that they are lost as the child carries them home. Or it may have been the termite, not the mouse. Small matter.

In Marcia's case, however, the principle of balance had been shelved, ignored, not to say flouted. Not even the temporary form of stinginess to which the young are normally subjected had been employed. (And in case you had forgotten its workings, see Commodus again in his tadpole phase.) Eleven, twelve, thirteen are the years for marriage in girls maybe, but they are also the years for pimples and greasy skin and uncontrolled limbs and uncontrolled laughter. Marcia's skin was as smooth as a sheet of gold, her body belonged to her and played her no tricks, her intelligence, weighty and potentially unmanageable, was directed constantly outwards. You would never catch her asking herself, as I have seen most brilliant youngsters do, as I have done in my time myself, What is this person thinking of me? Rather her question was, What is this person thinking? Is the thought interesting? Where does it lead and is it worth my while pursuing it? (Although the laugh, to tell the truth, *was* a little raucous at times.) Such command could have been daunting, such a wealth of gifts annoying – particularly to her contemporaries. But somehow it was not; somehow, young and old alike, people felt happy in her company, happy and at ease and glad to know her. It was her crowning gift – the chowder, so to speak, with which a master cook tops his dish before sending it to table – that she did not attract envy in anyone who knew her except of the most remote and perfunctory kind. Even Lucilla and Crispina when it came to it resented her position, I think, more than her actual person. They wanted to be rid of her for what she represented and set themselves to achieve this goal with all the means at their disposal, but face to face with her they too came under the spell.

Because the spell, you must understand, was irresistible and universal: plants felt it, animals felt it – I remember how even in their cages in our underground workroom the birds would brighten as she entered, and sing for her, and preen their feathers. Children felt it, men felt it, women felt it. Faustina felt it. Marcus felt it. Commodus felt it . . .

'And you felt it yourself.' Cassius's intervention is made slyly, with a trace of prurience, as if he had made a faintly shameful discovery capable of accounting for all sorts of things. It seems a pity to disappoint him by meeting it with absolute candour, but disappoint him I must.

'Yes, Excellency, and I felt it myself.' And like a huntsman with an over-keen puppy I remove the Senator's nose firmly from the promising but utterly false trail and try to get him to pick up the correct one.

The scent is subtler, of course, and more difficult to follow. I have some trouble in identifying it myself. I fell not only under Marcia's spell, I fell deeply in love with her. Just as I fell deeply in love with Commodus too, eventually, when he had stopped being a tadpole and had turned into something closer to a god. Perhaps more deeply, to be honest, because more of my handiwork had gone into his making. But neither emotion rivalled or even approached the plunging, vorticose, abyss-like depth of my love-affair with the Project itself with which these two young people were associated in my mind, and over which I was now – suddenly, without warning, without even wanting to be, really – placed in a position of more or less absolute control.

The enthusiasm which any mention of the Project is still able to awaken in me is cut short by a kind of puffing sound.

'Another story?'

It is Cassius again, by now becoming more than a little restless. The massage is beginning to pall, the chickens are beginning to squawk, I have disappointed him over the incest, and my spending so many words on what is to him at the end of it all only a vulgar concubine and an eleven-year-old concubine at that, has just about drained his patience.

Nor can I blame him really. I may have enjoyed giving my description of Marcia, but I am the first to see that there is no life to it, no breath, not a trace of the real person it is supposed to be about. I have fallen into the historian's trap myself, giving my character all the virtues and making her sound like a plaster statue.

'No, Excellency,' I reassure him, giving him a last wipe-down and putting away my ointments, 'not another story. We are finished with stories for today.'

'Ah,' says Cassius, rising and making flapping noises with his towel, I trust in the direction of the chickens. 'Another story tomorrow, then?'

I remain bland and reassuring. 'No, Excellency, not another story tomorrow either. The same story but another chapter of it. A chapter all about love. Your Excellency should relish that, surely, a chapter about love?'

Cassius puffs again and says that what he would really relish from now on, thank you very much, is brevity. He has appreciated these talks of ours, not to mention the medical treatment, but alas time is running short: as I will probably have heard, his assignment has been made final now, he is due to leave the city in a few days' time and has a hundred-and-one things to do before he goes, and I still haven't got round to tackling the question of the parricide which, after the incest, is the only thing left which truly interests him. Could we not therefore skip the love tomorrow and go straight to the hatred?

We could, I reply, of course we could. If His Excellency could show me a coin that has only one face to it, or a dish that has no underside, or a cloth that has no reverse.

'The two things were that intimately connected?'

The Senator has not quite grasped my meaning but he has come close enough. I assent. 'The two things, Excellency, are always that intimately connected.'

STUDIA ADOLESCENTIAM ALUNT, SENECTUTEM OBLECANT

(If by this Cicero means: Study is good for the young but only the old actually enjoy it, then I hope I proved him wrong.)

People often compare their love to fire. Not poets or writers, I mean, but ordinary people when struck by its extraordinary force. Although rough and plain and unfit for literary use, the metaphor seems to come to us naturally. Our passions scorch us or warm us, fuel us or destroy us; they flare up, they die down; they blaze for an instant or smoulder for years. Even those who are little acquainted with the matter and have only felt the heat with the tips of their fingers, so to speak, or singed the ends of their whiskers in it in passing will agree that this is the way it is: painful or comforting, short or enduring, lethal or life-giving, love is a fire.

In the course of my triple love-affair – with Marcia, Commodus and the Project – I burnt in the fire myself at maximum heat for a period of, I would say, four-and-a-half to five years, perhaps more; after which I continued to roast in it at slightly lesser temperatures for another fifteen or thereabouts, and still lie among its embers today, which are still capable of affording me warmth or discomfort, depending. Thus, despite the gallons of water which have meanwhile been poured on it and the numerous firebreaks with which it has been fought (not least those very real and daunting ones blazed by Severus – fire against fire in the best Roman tradition), it has proved itself as far as I am concerned to be a great and powerful bonfire indeed.

Understand me well. I am not and never have been a lover of adolescents in the commonplace physical sense, and I am not and never have been a natural teacher. The nape of Commodus's neck, the wonderfully serious cast of his features as he grappled with a problem he couldn't compass, the clean smell of puppies' feet that came from his clothing, Marcia's frown, or her eyes when the mind behind them was lit and I could see it shining through in quest of mine – these things would sometimes catch at my heartstrings and make my pulse run quicker, else I would have no right to say that I loved at all. But I think I can also say, and in all honesty, that it was *only* the heartstrings that were thus involved, and that the other strings less pretty to name remained largely unaffected throughout the entire course of our friendship. Unlike Socrates I can claim no merit for this: I won no battles against my evil demon, I simply had none to fight. And as regards the matter of the teaching, I have taught all my life, but purely incidentally, because I have had information to impart and feel it is my duty to pass it on. The only part of it I enjoy, as can be seen from my zest in the anatomy lessons in the ice cellar, is teaching people things that I myself do not know. Which scarcely qualifies me as a good pedagogue.

Mine was not a fire of the senses, therefore, and it did not feed itself on any recognizable form of professional pride, and it was consequently purer and consequently hotter than any other I have ever felt. Like all good blazes it began gradually. For one thing, as I think I have already explained, Marcus was slow to reveal to me the full extent and nature of his Project. For another, although I fell for Marcia immediately, I was slow to take to Commodus, and both Commodus and Marcia were even slower to take to me – and I cannot say I blame them. And finally there was the above question of the teaching, which, even when I was ravished by its theoretical side, continued, in its practical everyday implications like choosing texts or inspecting written work or simply listening to Pitholaus's evening summaries of how the day had gone, to bore me to dust. As it always has done and always will. (And that is at least one advantage which old age has brought me now I come to think of it: a decline in the number of my unlovely medical students.)

There were bursts, outbreaks of flame, sudden rises in the temperature; few falls, or few that I can think of. The cracking of the writing problem marked a rise. Marcia's arrival among us a few weeks later marked a rise. Pitholaus's conversion to my method, which came shortly afterwards marked a rise – largely because it freed me from day-in, day-out attendance in the schoolroom and made me better tempered: with another to do the donkey-work, I had more time to devote to my profession. And there were various other things too which helped to kindle my enthusiasm for the Project in these early stages, not least the fact that Marcus, whose departure for the northern front was now pending and could no longer be delayed, chose this time to discuss his plan with me in greater depth than he had ever done before or was ever to do again. Partly, I suppose, because he had had to.

He still didn't show me, mind you, the full extent to which the Project ran in his mind – this would have been difficult when there were in fact no boundaries to it. And knowing my limits as a teacher he still did not go into all the thousand-and-one practical details it involved – these were to come later by letter, list after list of them, dwarfing the quite extraordinarily long list I already had and embracing every aspect of the two children's lives, from diet to sleeping habits (the question of the blankets raised again: one, if I insisted, but plain wool, undyed – no furs, no feathers), to study and deportment and manners and even pronunciation and which words it was seemly for my pupils to use and which not. But no, on this occasion with a cunning that was unusual to him he showed me the pure and utter beauty of his idea, untrammelled by measurements, uncomplicated by the mechanics of its application. The Form of it, as Plato himself would have said. The essence. The light.

We sat there, I recall, in that curious little cell-like room that was his study (and if I had once thought it an affectation on the part of a Head of State to adopt this retreat – so mean and remote and badly serviced – now, I felt so no longer. Coming as I did from the main buildings of the Palace where preparations for the next day's departure had reached fever pitch, it was like entering a harbour in a storm). We sat there, then, myself on the floor where I felt more comfortable, Marcus perched like a scribe on a stool, and stiltedly at first, but with more and more enthusiasm as he went along until in the end he was bubbling with excitement like a child, Marcus at last opened up to me this further and very central compartment of his mind. He granted me, that is, a glimpse of the Vision.

And the Vision kindled me? Cassius enquires dubiously here, speaking into my ear-hole, almost. Either as a courtesy now that our conversations are coming to an end, or else simply to speed things up and get them over with, he has dispensed me from massage and has ordered a second couch to be brought, so today we lie side by side in the afternoon sunlight, quite like old friends.

Oh very much so, I confirm. Marcus in private and on topics that interested him could in his strange, awkward, rather remote way be a very rousing speaker when he chose. The delivery was never good, but he had artistry with words. As his Journals in my opinion testify. I can hear him now, his voice charged with feeling, the stutter which he shared with his son swept away like flotsam on the wave of his speech, as he described to me what he saw in his mind. And not only, but what we both of us would see in the flesh if we performed our task correctly. Provided, of course, that the 'flesh' we had to work on proved to be of the right quality: something of which he confessed himself to be still unsure.

'Imagine, Galen, a man not only born, but reared and nurtured to become a leader of others. A man who is a stranger from birth to greed or personal ambition; who has everything and consequently craves for nothing; who has no aim in life, no desire save that of furthering the well-being of the people over whom he is placed. Think, only think what such a man could do. What benefits he could bring to his subjects. What wrongs he could right. What service he could render. What works he could perform. He must be worldly-wise, of course, must know how to choose his counsellors, must learn how to read men's souls – even the ugly passages which they try to keep hidden. Above *all* the ugly passages, you will no doubt say, my friend, and you may be right. But so long as he is able to come by this wisdom in such a way as to leave his own heart uncorrupted (which is really what the process of education we must now attempt is all about); provided he is able to do this, just picture to yourself, Galen, if you can, the immeasurable, incalculable amount of good that a man with these qualities would be able to do. In terms of justice. In terms of peace. In terms of social cleanliness. In terms of order, righteousness, morality. In terms of anything of value that you care to name.'

I give only a tiny sample of Marcus's oratory – in actual fact his ideas were far cloudier and wispier and took much longer than this to state – but hopefully enough to show Cassius that it was indeed stuff capable of firing the passions. For who could fail to be moved by such a powerful and yet at the same time simple and viable recipe for bringing harmony to this dissonant world? Certainly not I, whose mind has an organizational bent and who have dreamt from the cradle dreams of power, well used and well directed. No wonder, then, that I begin to warm to the idea.

The most significant rise in temperature, however, I now go on to explain to Cassius. I trace, funnily enough, not to that intense and agitated evening of revelations (important though it undoubtedly was to the ends of my involvement, because after all, despite what His Excellency may feel about them, a Vision is a Vision and one is not granted many in the course of a life), but to the morning after when Marcus left. It was then, I think, that the fire really caught on and really began to burn. Perhaps – I do not know, but perhaps because responsibility is to me an essential condition for involvement, and independence an essential condition of responsibility, and both so far had been lacking.

I stood there, close to the main gate of the Palace, watching the last of the wagons which composed the imperial train trundle through, marvelling to myself how so much mass and might should leave behind it as its only sign of passage a scattering of horse-dung, and can remember feeling – so fiercely that I can almost feel it even now – a great flare of excitement rise up inside me at the prospect of the task that lay ahead. The illness which had struck Commodus, delaying like this our departure, seemed as then a trivial one, already on the point of clearing up. I counted therefore on having only a month or two of regency over the Project, six at the outside, certainly nothing approaching the stretch of time I was in fact to be granted by circumstance. But even so, the thought of what was being offered to me, the thought – not of the power so much as the scope and the possibilities that were now mine if only I knew how to make use of them, went to my head. No, forgive me, my head had been conquered already, the evening before by Marcus: went to my heart.

So I *was* responsible. Of course I was, I was responsible for everything. For four-and-a-half years. And for what is more, four-and-a-half plastic, pliable, formative years. Marcus sent letters, instructions, counsels; I read them, I heeded them, I did not always follow them. Marcus showed me his dream; I heeded that also, but I dreamt on my own account as well. He gave me the single recipe, for one individual; I doubled it, squared it, making provisions for a dynasty. I won't say I went so far as to disregard Plato's original to which I was supposed in Marcus's intentions continuously to refer for guidance, but I often mixed it with a strong dose of common sense, and this did, I admit, mean a certain alteration to its content.

Plato, for example, unlike Cassius shows a great respect for Visions and the like and lays much stress on their importance for the future ruler. According to him, before being capable of leading his subjects in the right direction the Philosopher-King must have been granted a kind of mystical sighting of Goodness, Righteousness in its most naked and absolute form; otherwise, in this world of traps and shadows he will scarcely know where it is located or which *is* the right direction.

Poetic, and possibly feasible for the head of a small rural community such as a Greek king of the time would have been, but nonsensical in my view for a leader of today's churning and multifarious world, populated by hundreds of conflicting groups of people clamouring for hundreds of conflicting things. I wanted my pupils, both of them, to be good, responsible people, and I did everything in my power to make them so and I think I succeeded; but above and beyond this I wanted them to be able to make practical and level-headed decisions for the general welfare of their subjects. Or what they considered, using again the reliable yardstick of common sense, to be the general welfare of their subjects. Capacity which as can be seen very clearly in the matter of the Sea-Snakes, often entails using a measure of what at the time may appear to be harshness, even ruthlessness, but without which leadership is quite simply not leadership at all.

Take gardening, for example (a discipline very close to statecraft when you come to think of it). Imagine a nurseryman who never had the heart to prune his plants or hack away the deadwood; who was afraid to get his hands dirty, who couldn't plan ahead, couldn't dig, couldn't burn the rubbish, couldn't stamp out pests; worse still, couldn't even tell the flowers from the weeds. What sort of a garden would such a man end up with? With a wilderness, that's what. Just as in my own profession, a doctor who did not know how to bleed and purge and cauterize and wield the knife when the knife was called for, would eventually find himself surrounded by nothing but death and disease. Such being the case I was anxious, yes, for my two young aspiring gardeners to learn the tender crafts of planting and nourishing and caring for their crops. But I was every bit as anxious, if not more so, for them to master the use of the hoe and the plough and the harrow and the scythe. *And* for them to develop a keen eye for weeds – especially in the early stages when it is easier to root them up. *And* to learn how to drive a clean furrow. *And* to accustom themselves to the raw feel of earth under their nails. I have probably said this already, but at the risk of repeating myself: leadership is *not* for the squeamish.

A word or two now about how I set about realizing the Project on the practical plane and how I conducted it and developed it. For Cassius's information, yes, but also because the period was a magical one for me and I take pleasure in recalling it.

With the departure of Marcus – a massive remove this time which everyone knew was to be lengthy – the Palace reverted almost immediately to a state of what I can only describe as anarchy. Although the term is not quite correct: there was a rule of sorts, exercised mainly I think by the ringleaders of the mysterious subterranean network which the Washer was later to warn me so fervently against disturbing. This underground power, if such it was, lost no time, but with the last horse hardly out of the gates and the dung on the road still fuming, surfaced from the burrows where it had been hiding and took over. Each day as I walked through the various suites of rooms on my way to my pupils' apartments I would come across groups of strange, ragged, rough-looking people I had never seen before – generally shepherded, I will admit, by someone whose face I did know and who smiled at me reassuringly to show that things were in order – engaged in all sorts of curious activities, like rummaging through bundles of linen, or sawing busily through piles of wood, or carting crockery, or briskly concluding bargains with spits and handclaps. Those few members of the permanent staff who had remained behaved differently, even walked differently; held their heads higher, took their time over things, and strode around as if they owned the place. Which I suppose, occupation being the greater part of ownership, in a sense they did. It became increasingly difficult to obtain service, even for Commodus in his sickroom.

Now I am a born organizer, that much should be clear by now, and I love a battle. But only when there is a chance of winning, and here there was evidently none. Instead of raising complaints, therefore, and also because I thought the change of air would do Commodus good, I left the guardians of the Palace to their profitable affairs, and as soon as Commodus was fit to travel, transferred our own little household – twenty-seven of us I think there were counting the slaves (and it was part of the children's programme of education, and one Marcus set much store by, that one *must* count the slaves) – to the smallest and what had always seemed to me nicest and most convenient of the imperial residences – a low, rambling old country-style villa lying in the midst of a tiny residual oak wood on the slopes of the Caelian hill.

The house was Marcus's birthplace and his childhood home, and although he had never to my knowledge used it since, nor lent it, nor rented it, he had always kept it on, fully staffed, and had carried out the necessary repairs – I presume for sentimental reasons. Certainly, when in order to raise money for the wars he made his grand gesture of stripping himself of all his possessions and auctioning them to the public, he was careful that this particular possession should not figure on the list. (But then, nor did many others, so one may say that the gesture was anyway somewhat incomplete.) Eventually, of course, the villa was to be Commodus's and Marcia's deathplace too. But of that we were all of us as yet fortunately unaware.

I was right about the air. Commodus's health came back immediately, almost the moment we entered the grounds, and remained good in the main for the entire length of our stay.

'And how long was that, if I may ask?' Cassius interrupts me. Perhaps because there is no more massage to lull him, the Senator's attention today is sharp again. I am not sure I don't prefer it blunted.

I tell him I have mentioned the duration already: four-and-a-half years. This appears to puzzle him, as well it might. But if the boy's health remained good, he asks reasonably but not disguising his scepticism, then why didn't I accompany him north to be reunited with his father and mother and the rest of the family as arranged? Was it that I had meanwhile become so possessive of the Project that I could brook no interference? And if so, then how did I get away with this as far as the Emperor was concerned? Didn't Marcus Aurelius require explanations? Didn't he keep checks on me? Didn't he send observers to find out what was going on? Admittedly doctors can always argue their way round anything, but all the same, four-and-a-half years are four-and-a-half years . . .

Cassius sidesteps the tautology by making the second four-and-a-half years sound like aeons, which of course they were not. But even so, I grant that four-and-a-half years would indeed have been a long time wilfully to keep a son separated from his father. However, as I now do my best to explain to the Senator, there was nothing wilful about the matter at all. I was, yes, jealous of my independence over the Project. I did, yes, become more and more jealous as time progressed. So much so that when it finally came to our leaving the villa and rejoining Marcus I made excuses and remained behind in Rome because, quite apart from the fact that I do not much like campaigning or leaving my practice for long in the hands of others, I just could not face the thought of conducting things henceforth on another man's terms, however similar they might be to mine. But the reason for our long permanence in the villa had nothing to do with this, it was simply that in obedience to some strange mechanism I have never been able to fathom, every single time we got ready to travel – and despite my growing reluctance, in the course of the first year or so anyway we did so quite often: got all packed up and seated ourselves in the wagons and sometimes journeyed for as long as three or four hours before having to turn back – every time we did this Commodus's illness would make a violent reappearance. His breathing would become laboured, he would wheeze, sneeze, catch at his chest, cough, and his eyes would start to water and his face to take on that nasty bluish tinge which is one of the heralds of suffocation, so that there was no choice but for me to halt the carriage immediately and hustle him out into the fresh air until the fit passed and he regained his normal colour.

Under such conditions travelling was impossible, and after one last attempt, which Marcus insisted on our making and which ended close to disaster with Marcia in tears and myself flat on the ground beside Commodus trying in desperation to pump air into him from my own mouth (merely succeeding in badly chipping one of his front teeth: I should have known better than to think I could do another person's breathing for them), we stayed put where we were, in the villa.

Where the disease did not visit the child? Cassius intervenes again, the note of scepticism still tainting his voice.

Where the disease did visit the child, I tell him, but only rarely, and only when there were either carriages or horses in the vicinity. I am unable to be more precise about it; the thing baffled me then and it baffles me still. It was a travelling complaint, evidently, a complaint which affects only voyagers. And to add to its mystery it disappeared as suddenly as it came. When the four-and-a-half years were up and my pupils finally set off on the long voyage to rejoin their father and family, although I was not accompanying them all the way I purposely rode with them more than a quarter of the distance, watching over Commodus like a hawk the entire time, and was relieved to see that he was totally free of all his previous symptoms. Nor did they ever to my knowledge come back to afflict him again. So besides being a travellers' disease, it was a youthful travellers' disease, circumscribed to a certain very well defined phase of the development.

'A convenient phase, Galen, so far as you were concerned.'

Oh, no, His Excellency is wrong, *not* convenient. The period, as I have already said, was magical. Although I use the word laxly: nothing depresses me more than magic in real life. What I mean is that I lived as men are said to do when in thrall of an enchanter but doubtless do not, i.e. in a state of constant delight. I have spoken of the fierce delights of the fire, but what I have not yet described are the gentle delights of peace and regularity and order which our life in the villa now enabled me to taste. It was a flavour I was not accustomed to and was not often to taste again.

Our days passed in the following manner. We would rise at dawn, all of us, slaves included, and before carrying out our toilets we would gather together in the only sizeable room the villa boasted – or on the patio outside when it was warm, under the vine – and would eat our morning meal and drink our morning bowl of water. There was a spring in the wood and the water was some of the best I have ever tasted; a bit laxative in its effect, which meant a rush to the lavatory if you wanted to beat the tutors and get a good seat, but otherwise ideal for the health.

This opening interlude was Marcus's idea and was intended by him to be one of conviviality and conversation: he was particularly anxious that Commodus should not develop his own tendency to morning laziness, and particularly anxious also that at least once a day the slaves be treated on a par with the other members of the household *by* the other members of the household. In his enthusiasm, however, Marcus seemed to have overlooked the fact that morning laziness is a tendency common to most, and of conversation I am afraid there was generally very little. Nevertheless, if we sat in silence we sat in comfortable silence – until the water began to take its effect, that is – and we continued these early-morning meetings throughout our stay.

When the business of eating and evacuating was over we would

separate and go to our several toilets while the slaves got down to
their work. Then Commodus and Marcia would begin their lessons,
and I would be free for the rest of the morning to attend to my
own affairs: my patients, my school, my studies, my experiments,
whichever were the most pressing. Usually, of course, the patients,
because my guardianship over Commodus had given a great boost
to my prestige and I was much in demand.

I would not return to the villa until midday, when, in reduced
company this time, just my charges and myself, we would eat another
light meal. Then I would perhaps study on my own for a little longer
while Commodus and Marcia took exercise according to the Platonic
handbook and went to the baths. (Because it was the first time I had
lived in a house which afforded me real privacy and I wanted to
make the best of it.) Or else I would go to the baths with them
(because it was also the first time I had lived in a house with its
own independent complex of baths and I wanted to make the best
of that too). Or else, sometimes, unheard of for me before and since,
I would sit in the sun and watch the cats and the lizards and do nothing.
Without falling asleep, though, because another charm of the villa,
perhaps its greatest, was that it was sufficiently isolated for one not
to be kept awake at night by the delivery wagons and the cries of the
carters unloading their wares.

(I am not sure, but I fancy I hear Cassius at this point murmur
another 'convenient', in none too sympathetic a tone. However, I do
not take him up on it. If he still knows so little about me as to think I
am influenced by material comforts then he had better go ahead and
think it.)

The time which remained before supper – our main meal, this,
taken with Pitholaus, the better-mannered of the tutors, and Savia,
Marcia's formidable nurse-cum-companion-cum-dresser who I tried
to exclude from the company, registering my only failure over discipline in the entire stay; these two or three precious hours before
supper, then, would be spent in what I myself considered to be
education proper. My own education, that is, in all senses. What
I thought it important for my pupils to learn, and what I thought
it important for me to learn myself – with them, through them, for
them. Or sometimes, because they were after all very young at the
time and a little toe-dragging at that age is only natural, in spite of
them.

Always following the Platonic guideline that in acquiring knowledge nothing is to be taken for granted, but otherwise without fettering ourselves by any particular rule or method or timetable, we would address ourselves quite simply to whichever aspect of the cosmos happened to catch our attention on the day. The anatomy and workings of living things figured large, of course, because that was my own particular hobbyhorse, and unless and until they are taught to despise it, children have a great feeling for the animal world. But subjects have a way of running into one another when you tackle them with an open mind, and from there we would pass to the world of men and ideas, to history, poetry, the stars, love, hate, justice and injustice; to memory and why elephants and camels have such good ones, to whether the tiger can be termed evil when he kills, to what the horizon is made of and if a ship can ever reach it, to the power of limpets, the properties of spittle, what constitutes a duty, and why games are fun. We would study numbers and see what we could do with them, and geometry (which I knew very little about and which therefore fascinated me). We would discuss music and try to discover why it was superior to noise. We would visit the prisons sometimes and try to find out more about criminals. We would visit the Washer. We would roam the streets and talk to people. We would bring people in to talk to us. We would comb the wood in search of mushrooms and then set ourselves to sorting the good from the poisonous by dint of feeding them to snails and watching which ones died. (Although I must add I was never really sure enough about the method for us to act on it.)

Cassius has been listening to all this in audibly mounting surprise. Now he can check his surprise no longer.

'Mushrooms!' he says. 'Did I hear you aright? You gave your pupils mushroom lessons?'

I did, yes indeed, I confirm. And very profitable they were too because Commodus like his father had a real passion for mushrooms. Both to eat and to study. In adult life, apart from the evenings spent with Marcia and myself in the underground laboratory, it was about the only distraction he allowed himself: a walk through the woods now and again on spring and autumn mornings in search of his beloved sponges and witches' fingers and gold pies, or whatever it was he used to call them. He could no longer eat what he picked, of course, his enemies had grown too numerous by then, but even so he loved just going out with his stick and his dogs and hunting around.

In early childhood the passion had needless to say been frowned on by Pitholaus, who was convinced that the handling of mushroom stalks led to priapism. (I wish it did. Just think of the money a doctor could make!) But when I took charge I encouraged it, and I think rightly, since it was in fact while watching my pupil busy in this pursuit: observing, sorting, naming, dividing his booty into families on the basis of resemblance, that my remaining fears about his intelligence were finally put to rest. (Because, oh, yes, despite what I said to Marcus I did still harbour one or two, and for quite a long time. It was hard not to when the handwriting continued so wobbly and perverse.) The book which was the outcome of his labours was not a very lovely one, and bristled with blots and crossings-out and spelling mistakes, but nevertheless it was clear to me the moment I saw it that no boy of his age could have produced such a full and comprehensive survey as this without having all his wits about him. Somewhere. I sent the volume to Marcus in triumph but unfortunately it was lost on the way and never reached him.

Mine is not a malleable character, of course, and sometimes in the choice of subject I would do a certain amount of guiding: steering my pupils' attention away from those topics I thought we had been into quite deeply enough (because mushrooms, however varied, have their limits to my mind as objects of study) and leading it, occasionally pushing it, towards others less immediately alluring. Sometimes I would not even guide but choose outright. Science, after all, is my mistress, and it would have been foolish of me – unforgivably foolish – if I had not now and again taken advantage of my position in order to attend to her needs as well as my pupils'. For instance, there was a certain assertion made by Plinius Secundus – the same Plinius I referred to earlier on, the writer and volcano victim – in which it is stated with tranquil assurance that the only known substance in the world capable of disintegrating a diamond is goats' blood. Now, how could I, I ask you, placed for the first and perhaps last time in my life in a position where I could come by an expendable diamond, resist the urge to put this assertion to the test?

In the main, however, I neither pushed nor pulled, and only very seldom imposed my will on my pupils like this. (And I knew they would enjoy the business of the diamond anyway, children have a very proper sense of values.) Becoming increasingly aware, the more time I spent with them and the more liberty I granted, that their young brains were usually capable of coming up with better questions, even, than my own. The Project loomed, of course, bestrode my thoughts and dominated my affections; it was what I lived for, and what drove me forward. But for much of what I call the enchantment of the period, intellectual and otherwise, it was them I have to thank really – my pupils, my poor dead pupils and their life-giving questions.

NON VIRTUTE HOSTIUM, SED AMICORUM PERFIDIA DECIDI

(In the words of Cornelius Nepos, changing them a bit because it would be wrong in this case to speak of perfidy: Not to the strength of my enemies do I owe my ruin, but to the weakness of my friends.)

Thinking back on what was such a pleasant period in my life, I have evidently got carried away and forgotten the time. Now I realize it is late and growing chilly. It must be nearly supper-time.

I ask Cassius if he would like me to stop here and finish my story tomorrow, but he calls for blankets and says that having gone so far I may as well continue. He never sups until the last hen has bedded down. He still can't see, though, he adds, where the parricide fits into all this.

Unfortunately, I tell him, it fits all too snugly. And suppressing my hunger (because with the Senator's views on protocol I think it unlikely I will be invited to share his meal), I pick up my story where I left off.

From the moment I took charge of it I had anticipated, feared all kinds of threats to the Project from all kinds of directions. I had feared Commodus's inadequacy, feared that Marcia might tire of her role of pacemaker, feared the tutors would contest me or let me down or in some way undermine what I was trying to bring about, feared illness, incompatibility, everything – from bee stings (which had a terrible effect on Commodus, almost worse than the journeys) to earthquakes. I had even, briefly, feared that I myself might prove not quite up to the task I had been assigned.

Then when these fears proved themselves groundless I had had others, for the future. First the journey itself: for what if Commodus's illness did return after I had left and my substitute lost his head and was unable to cope? What if the horses went berserk? What if the carriage overturned in the mountains and fell down a ravine? What if it snowed? What if the company was attacked by wolves? Journeys are terrible things, even with the routes as well monitored as they are today. Then the arrival: the war, the diseases again – encampments crawl with them, the fighting, the enemy, and worse than the enemy, the Emperor's so-called 'friends' – the courtiers, that is, and the scheming and faction-forming and rivalry that went on between them on every side and in every corner. I even feared the Empress, and with reason, having just been informed by my Chief-Assistant who was acting as deputy for me to the travelling Court and came by all the gossip, about her recent involvement in a plot to overthrow the Emperor and how her treachery had been discovered by Marcus and thwarted (and then, of course, as I also mentioned earlier on, patched over and forgiven). Because a woman who was ready to scheme against her own husband merely because he had ceased to give her the necessary reassurance, what would she not do against her son – who, if things went as planned when he took over the reins of government, would almost certainly give her very little reassurance indeed?

What had not crossed my mind, however, in the midst of this busy traffic of worries and suspicions, was that the most dangerous threat to the enterprise would come from Marcus himself. That was one possibility – and perhaps the only one – that I had not foreseen. Distance, they say, turns men into strangers, but despite the miles and the years there had been no distance between the Emperor and myself that I was aware of. Marcus's letters had arrived regularly, mine had answered them, we had remained in touch and in harmony throughout the entire four-and-a-half-year period and had consulted one another over every question that arose more or less as it arose. The post was not quite as swift then as it is now: Marcus did not drive men or horses the way Severus does, but under normal conditions we were able to get a message through to one another in just under four days, and generally did so, at least twice weekly if not more. My own letters, what is more, being written at leisure and not, like Marcus's, under the stress of warfare, were very full and explicit. I don't think that I kept anything from him really – anything of importance, that is, anything weightier than the blankets and other trivialities of the kind. And when I went my own way, as I so often did, and made my common-sense modifications to the programme and ironed out some of its more fanciful Platonic frills, I was always careful to inform him of the fact and, where possible, to gain his consent beforehand. Thus he was not only aware of the progress that both pupils had made, and what point they had reached in their education, but he knew of the deep feelings that each had developed for the other and professed to approve of them – very strongly. He shared my enthusiasm, my hopes, my fears; he knew my mind and what was going through it; he knew more or less everything and agreed with it wholeheartedly.

Or so I thought. Written messages, of course, no matter how many and how detailed, tend to be a poor substitute for reality, and I understand from what Marcia and Commodus told me later that when they reached the camp and were ushered into their father's presence the actual meeting between them was fraught with surprise and unease – particularly on the side of Marcus, who did not even recognize his son to begin with but amidst general embarrassment stepped forward to embrace one of the pages instead: as luck would have it, a twelve-year-old Sardinian with a squint and bandy legs. But even so, Marcus was still at this stage the linchpin around which the entire Project revolved; despite my growing jealousy it was still very much *his* Project, he was still in apparent sympathy with it even if he had temporarily lost contact with, shall we say, certain rather important aspects of its realization, and his heart was consequently the very last place in the entire universe and beyond from which I would have expected an attack to come.

And yet when it came that was precisely where it came from: from Marcus's own heart. Not his head, because, I repeat, I prefer to think that the head was already contaminated by then and no longer properly speaking a part of him, but his heart.

The danger was not visible immediately, mind you; for six or seven months after my pupils' departure I continued to receive letters from both of them in a tranquil, humdrum vein, telling me of what they were doing, how their health was faring, how they were adapting or not adapting to camp life, giving me news of the local inhabitants, the fauna, the vegetation and other things they thought would interest me (whole scrolls from Commodus, as you can imagine, dedicated to the abundant northern funghi). I received letters from Marcus also over the same period, three in all: the first congratulatory, ecstatic ('You promised me, Galen, an heir who would not disgrace me. You never told me you were sending me grace itself' etc., etc.), the other two quieter but still echoing thanks and displaying a flattering amount of wonder at my achievement. The Emperor seemed to derive nothing but pleasure from his son's transformation, and pronounced himself full of plans for the future – bold, radical, optimistic plans, none of them deviating very widely from the similarly bold and radical lines we had already laid down. Although I do seem to remember him expressing doubts about the abolition of the family and the new methods of breeding and child-raising we had decided to introduce in its stead, which I suppose should have warned me of the drift his mind was taking. Neither he nor Commodus nor Marcia made any mention of Faustina's little slip-up.

The seventh month, however, brought a break in the correspondence. Break which to begin with did not trouble me. I knew that the situation at the front was quieter, I knew also, because he had stated this clearly in his last message to me, that Marcus was taking advantage of the quiet to leave the camp and travel south again, making a detour to the east as well while he was about it in order to show Commodus and Marcia those parts of their future empire which they had never seen. I attributed the silence therefore to the journey itself: anyone who has ever travelled beyond his own cabbage-patch knows how slight the inclination is, at sundown, when the jolting stops, to take up a pen and write. And word having meanwhile reached me, again from my gossip-loving deputy, that another of Marcus's reasons for leaving the north was that the Empress had now fallen ill and had expressed a desire to undergo treatment in some fancy medical establishment in Syria or I know not where, when I didn't put the silence down to journeying I put it down – in Marcus's case at any rate – to worry.

Justifiable worry as it turned out. Only a few weeks later and my assistant wrote to me again, informing me of Faustina's death. It had taken place, so he said, quite gently as deaths go, before she even reached the School of Medicine to which she was directed. There was no suspicion of unnatural causes and no bandying of blame: the Empress had never been quite right since her last late confinement, bleeding often from the womb, and her symptoms had merely worsened progressively until she had stopped eating altogether and one by one her bodily functions had ceased. He attributed her demise himself, he said in his letter, to a cluster of small pebble-like objects which he had afterwards found in the gall bladder – very swollen, this, and lacerated and distended – and to the rattling of these against the walls of the gall bladder, provoked by the motion of the carriage.

Exactly how this material my assistant described could have got in to where it did I do not know, and neither, obviously, did he, but the condition being a well-known one, often present in sufferers from strangury, I tend to think his theory was correct and to rule out, as he did, any suspicion of foul play: poison, yes, but you certainly cannot administer gravel to people without their consent. Poor Faustina. Her courage in the face of death was apparently great – fact which I could well believe – and, still, according to my deputy, she paid me the ultimate homage of calling for me, almost with her very last breath. Disciples, however, will say anything to ingratiate themselves with their master, and this fact I am not sure I believe quite as firmly.

I wrote a long letter to Marcus on his bereavement, but apart from a brief note of acknowledgement, so stiff and formal that I hardly count it as communication, the silence continued unbroken on all three fronts – his, Commodus's and Marcia's. And now, I will admit, I *did* begin to find the thing a little strange. Not to say troubling. Not to say, also, more than a little wounding.

No amount of worrying, however, and of turning over possibilities in my mind one by one in my usual painstaking pathologist's way, could ever have prepared me for the shock that was in store for me when I learnt the true reason for this prolonged and ever-deepening silence on the imperial front.

The news came to me this time not even from my assistant, who clearly had no cause to think that such a frivolous and marginal matter would concern me, but from a comparative stranger – an officer of Marcus's staff returned to Rome by a quicker route on sick-leave. He it was who, speaking carelessly, a little salaciously, assuming no doubt that I had already heard talk of the business and found it as amusing as he did, took it on himself to deliver the first breath-sapping blow. We were discussing, as was only natural, the Empress's death. The Emperor, the man said, was bearing his loss as usual with great and exemplary fortitude, did I not agree? Bracing, no, to see a man reacting so well, so soon? Four weeks' mourning, and then the appointment of a concubine. And such a young and beautiful concubine too. He had spotted her himself once or twice around the camp: firm and glossy as a ripe piece of fruit still on the tree. Splendid, he thought it was, for the campaigners to see their leader showing such pluck in adversity. Good for the morale. And then there was talk of a bride for Commodus too – doubtless another little plum with the bloom still on her. It all made for good cheer. In the case of the concubine, the annulment of her adoption had raised a few eyebrows, of course, caused a bit of talk and a bit of resentment: for anyone but an emperor the legal proceedings involved would have taken years. But all said and done, an admirable gesture, and very well received, especially by the troops.

I think – I hope – that I received the news of Marcus's gesture well enough myself, for, although no actor, I too can wear a mask when it suits me: witness my conduct during the Condemnation ceremony. But inside me, I assure you, as the officer spoke and as the meaning of his words became clear to me, I felt as if someone had slashed me across the face with an ox-whip, or knocked my knees from under me with a metal bar, or tipped me into the olive-press and turned the screw. Unlike the soldiers, I didn't in the least object to Marcus annulling his daughter's adoption: indeed, it had always been agreed on between us that sooner or later this was a step that would have to be taken in order for her marriage to Commodus to take place. Still less did I object to him taking a concubine so soon after his wife's death: as I saw it, the regulation of this aspect of his life was his affair. But that the two things should be connected; that the concubine in question should be Marcia herself, I mean, and that Marcus should have rescinded the adoption *for the precise purpose* of dragging her into his bed with what in this case was truly deplorable haste – this sickened me, appalled me, smote me to the quick.

It was days before I could so much as think of the matter, let alone think of it with calm. The act was so gross, so cruel, so wantonly destructive that even had it been made by a far lesser man in a far less delicate situation, it would have been hard to sanction. Coming from Marcus, and at such a time, with the Project at the stage it had reached, and our hopes within a hair's breadth of achieving reality, it was quite simply so vile and incomprehensible that it made my bowels turn. With a stroke and for no discernible reason other than his own well-being, his own consolation, he appeared to have destroyed everything. Or if not destroyed it, made a very serious attempt to do so. To return to the architectural image I have used before, it was as if with the delivery of my pupils I had handed over to the Emperor with pride the concrete execution of his original plan – built on *two* pillars instead of one for extra safety, and as if he in turn had then expressed his thanks by snatching away from under the building one of the pillars on which it rested and, not content, slamming into the other one with a battering-ram on his way, indifferent as to whether or not it would withstand the crunch. Poor pillars. Poor Marcia. Poor Commodus.

And poor Galen as well. Later, of course, in the weeks that followed, as I lay felled on my couch with the pile of Marcus's letters beside me, trying to make sense of them – in the 'light', to use his own bitter expression, of present events, I managed to find an explanation which accounted for everything. Or more or *less* everything. But it took time and ingenuity on my part to do so, and meanwhile my esteem for Marcus suffered such damage that it in turn, afterwards, required a considerable amount of time and ingenuity to repair. (If ever the repair was total, which is a thing I sometimes doubt. The head can be brought to excuse by force of reason, not so the heart to forgive.)

The explanation hinges, as I think I may have already outlined, although not in detail and definitely not to Cassius, on the question of the incest, and on the Empress's last-minute remedy for repairing her initial mistake. Remedy which, when you come to examine it closely, is as elegant and compact as its originator. For if, as I am now certain they were, Commodus and Marcia were indeed brother and sister, and if, as I now realize she must have been, Faustina was secretly appalled by the turn events had taken and wished to straighten things out immediately before it was too late, then by palming her daughter off on Marcus in quality of concubine, it must be admitted to her credit that she accomplished various things at once, and in what was a virtually foolproof and irreversible manner. She accomplished her children's moral safety – on the formal plane at least, which was presumably what most concerned her – making marriage between them impossible from then on. No high-born man can ever marry an ex-concubine, that's for sure. She accomplished her daughter's social ruin, maybe, but, again, what would have carried more weight, her financial triumph. And last, as an added bonus, she also made sure that her husband was looked after, kept out of trouble, kept amused, kept warm at night, and also perhaps, in a rather curious and indirect way, kept faithful to herself. Or part of herself. The solution may well not have been Faustina's first choice, mind you. It occurs to me now, as I look back on things, that in order to avoid the humiliation of a confession she may have tried other solutions first, her little political 'indiscretion' very likely among them. Again, not a friendly hypothesis, but I think she may have felt, that is, when confronted by the awful spectacle of her son and daughter passionately in love with one another, on the brink of marriage and about to inherit what she had always considered not unreasonably to be 'her' Empire, with their father's blessing upon them and who knows what shower of curses in its wake, that the only way of loosing the snarl she had created was by violent overthrow of the entire house of the Aurelii. No Marcus, no Commodus, no marriage, no incest, no anything. Marcus, as I said, closed his eyes, burnt the incriminating letters and tried to forget the incident, so we shall never know, but certainly it is a possibility. However, whether the second, third or even fourth choice, the solution Faustina finally settled for, as she herself must have realized when she hit on it, was quite extraordinarily effective.

And here, at the risk of trying Cassius's patience even further and missing my own supper altogether, I find it necessary to stall in my narrative and to play for time. Because with all these reasonings and hypotheses I appear to have landed myself in a slight moral quandary. On the one hand, that is, I feel it is my duty to continue to prevent any mention of the word 'incest' reaching Cassius's ears, at the risk of losing my chronicler on the spot; on the other I also feel it is my duty to continue as long as I can to present Marcus's character to Cassius in a favourable light. And this I can scarcely do in the present case *without* mentioning the dreaded word: it being one thing to snatch away your son's betrothed from under his nose for purposes of the young couple's moral salvation, another to do so out of lust.

Fortunately, however, just as I begin to run my finger over the tips of its horns, trying to see which is the sharper and whether there is any way of passing in between them, I am rescued from my dilemma by Cassius himself. Brought up in the old school and himself something of a soldier, he finds no cause for censure in the Emperor's gesture, rather the opposite. They weren't officially betrothed yet, were they, he asks, Commodus and this Marcia creature? Well then, so what is there to make a fuss about? Young men may squeak and squeal and bare their teeth and raise their hackles, but paternal authority is absolute, and if a father takes a fancy to a woman whom the son also happens to covet, then no matter how unfortunate and irksome for the latter – or even for the woman for that matter – it is the father who has first choice. That is just the way of the world. Look at bulls, look at stags, look at bees and king bees. I say I considered Marcus Aurelius's action a threat to the success of the political Project he and I were trying to actuate, and was wounded by what I considered his betrayal of our shared ideal, but he cannot see that there is much substance in the accusation himself. The selection of a concubine, after all, is a private matter and has nothing to do with politics or philosophy or affairs of State. A bit of a comedown for the girl perhaps, and a pity all that time wasted like that over her education. A bit of a jolt for young Commodus too, if he had meanwhile become so fond of her. But otherwise, no, he thinks the Emperor's decision must have come simply as a good stiff lesson in Platonic discipline for both the young people concerned. Subject in which, from the sound of it, my own teaching had been hitherto somewhat deficient. So no more humming and hawing, please, and no more waffling on about the negligible problems of two pampered adolescents who were very lucky to have had from life all that they did. Time is short, and in spite of what I promised, the story is not. On to the parricide with all haste.

So there we are; this takes care of my dilemma with Cassius. My dilemma with Marcus and my pupil was unfortunately far less easy to resolve. All too sadly aware by now, thanks to what the officer had told me, that the reason for the silence of all three of my correspondents was shame – albeit a different kind of shame in each case – I wrote no more, but in a mood of suspended fury threw myself into my work and awaited their return. I could, I suppose, have written to Marcus requesting enlightenment, but I found I preferred the darkness. And anyway, such a request on my part might well have been taken by him as impertinence. I could have written to Commodus too. In fact I very nearly did, getting more than half-way through a miserable letter which I kept by me for days and then, after eroding it with corrections, threw away. But to Marcia, no: to Marcia I found I had nothing to say at all.

She was almost the first person I saw, however, when a full two months later I at last re-entered the Palace; prepared – the word is hardly the right one under the circumstances – to pay homage to my returning patron and resume my office.

As so often happens when someone else has committed a wrong-doing, it was I who felt cobwebs of guilt hanging over me, and I can remember walking through the familiar rooms (purged now of the traffickers and seemingly of a lot else besides) with my head half averted so as to spare myself the bother of greeting anyone, and not raising it, or not with intent to see anyway, until I was ushered into the audience hall. Whatever shape it took, I wanted the meeting between Marcus and myself to be over as soon as possible and I wanted nothing to interfere with this or claim my attention meanwhile.

Save for the guards the hall was empty: Marcus evidently did not share my haste. I found a sad significance, too, in the fact that he had chosen to receive me in this formal way with no private meeting between us beforehand: evidently he wanted no renewal of intimacy either. To preserve my calm, or my appearance of calm, because inside I was shaking like a poplar, I walked over to the window behind the dais on which the audience chair stood and after rubbing hard at the glass for some moments with the hem of my cloak – remarking to myself as I did so that the dirt was at least one thing that the traffickers appeared not to have bothered to remove – I looked through the pane and out into the garden beyond. And it was there, seated round a table among a group of four or five other young women, all of them heads bowed and engaged in some finicky task which I could not quite identify, that I saw Marcia. The new Marcia.

The spoiled Marcia also, or so it seemed. Marcus, in common with most other men of severely ascetic tastes, always liked his women to be highly decorated and over-groomed: Faustina, in fact, who knew this well, on those rare occasions when she wanted to please her husband, would trick herself out like a harlot on her way to a funeral. I was still a little reluctant, of course, to think of Marcia as 'belonging' to Marcus in this intimate sense (after all, I tried to convince myself, it was still possible, was it not, that the appointment as concubine was purely nominal? just a ruse, an expedient, a way of avoiding the worst?), but all the same I knew that he would have had her dressed for the part, and some change in her appearance I had therefore expected, and had braced myself accordingly.

But I had not expected or braced myself for anything like this. I opened the window, just to make sure I was not deceived by the glass. I could hardly believe that it was she – the same serious, dignified young woman who had left my tutelage less than a year ago. Talk of a funeral-bound harlot; this extravagant creature looked like a whole procession of them rolled into one. And as for her being the imperial concubine in name alone – well, I knew I could safely shelve *that* little theory now and let it gather dust! If Plato's doctrine could be bent to such use (although in fairness to the author, he was always careful to say that it could not), then here in the person of the new Marcia was *the* original form of concubinehood; the matrix, as it were from which the world took its meaning; the concubine, not to end, but to begin all others. Her hair was caught up and held in an amazing construction – solid and towering, like a party-pudding or a presentation dish of fruit. I could see no trace of its former substance nor imagine how it could possibly revert to it ever. Jewels flashed from every ringlet, every curl, giving the impression that the head underneath was crowned with frozen light. Her neck, which as with Commodus was perhaps the part of her body I had loved best to look on, was gone also, hidden from sight by a collar of gold and pearls, thick and deep as a yoke. From her ears dangled bells, ridiculous, eye-catching things big as real ones that you might use to summon a slave. These too shone like the collar and showed themselves on closer inspection to be studded with jewels. The rest of the body was wrapped in a cloak, less brilliant than the jewels, perhaps, but none the less of extraordinary opulence: a huge, rich cascade of furs, in strips of different colours, woven into one another so as to resemble the hide of some imaginary beast, and belted in at the waist by another great swag of pearls. If, as a child, in her ceremonial garb, Marcia had reminded me with tenderness of a corn-stack, now she reminded me with distaste of a magician's doll.

I looked and looked, and wished that I could look away, but found myself unable to do so: magician's dolls, as is well known, have a way of commanding the attention. My eyes went to the fingernails, always grubby with ink when I had known them, and I saw that they were long and pointed now, and gilded, in conformity to the vulgar fashion of the time which decreed – and indeed still decrees today, even more strongly – that wealth is indolence and that indolence must show. I saw the feet, encased in slippers of a fashion and workmanship unknown to me. I saw the wrists and ankles, weighted down with yet more gold and yet more jewels. I saw the hands, obscured by rings, as they moved elegantly, somewhat listlessly, about whatever task it was that she and the other women were engaged in. I saw all this, and, illogically perhaps, for slippers and paint and baubles by definition almost signify very little, but in my heart I said goodbye to Marcia, and goodbye to the Project. And made ready also, at the very same moment in which I would greet him with my mouth, to say goodbye to Marcus as well.

The noise of a dropped sword warning me now of his approach, I made to close the window and squared myself to meet him.

VELUT ÆGRI SOMNIA

(Like a sick man's dreams.)

On this his second-last day in Rome, Cassius can spare me very little of his time. Having purposely stopped at an interesting point the evening before, I am invited in for a quick morning visit and told to make myself comfortable among the packing cases and to go ahead with my story, but I am warned that I have under an hour in which to finish it. The Senator is expecting a whole row of important goodbye visitors, and will hoof me out without ceremony the moment the first one arrives.

Before picking up my narrative again, even if it takes up precious minutes, I think it a good idea to begin with some extracts from Marcus's famous Daybook, which he began to keep about this time. Or, as Cassius prefers to call it, Nightbook: he cannot, he says, imagine anyone thinking such thoughts in the light of the sun. Better than any words of mine they help give an insight into what was happening under the crust of the poor imperial skull.

Concerning the physical world:
– Look at everything that exists and observe that it is already in dissolution and change, and, as it were, putrefaction or dispersion.
– The rottenness of the matter which is the foundation of everything: water, dust, bones, filth . . .
– Such as bathing appears to thee – oil, sweat, dirt, filthy water, all things disgusting – so is every part of life and everything.
– How ridiculous is he who is surprised at anything which happens.
– As it happens to thee in the amphitheatre and such places, that the continual sight of the same things and the uniformity make the spectacle wearisome, so it is with the whole of life; for all things, above, below, are the same and from the same.

149

Concerning (if I read correctly) the bodies of those we love:
– All this is foul smell and blood in a bag.

Concerning the mental and spiritual world:
– Everything which belongs to the body is a stream, and what belongs to the soul is dream and vapour, and life is a warfare and a stranger's sojourn, and after-fame is oblivion.

Advice to those condemned to inhabit these worlds:
– Do not consider life a thing of any value.
– Wipe out imagination: check desire: extinguish appetite.
– Consider thyself to be dead, and to have completed thy life up to the present time.

Instructions as to where the only available consolation is to be found, i.e., in the contemplation of life's fortunate briefness:
– Observe how ephemeral and worthless human things are, and what was yesterday a little mucus, tomorrow will be mummy or ashes.
– A man's life is only a moment, and after a short time we are all laid out dead.
– Before long thou wilt be nobody and nowhere.
– How soon will time cover all things, and how many has it covered already.

Briefness which, however, is nowhere near sufficient for his own needs, since later we find:
– How long then?
– Enough of this wretched life and murmuring and apish tricks.
– Come quick, O Death.

And finally, what seems to me the most telling and most heartrending cry of all:
– It is a shame for the soul to be the first to give way in this life, when the body does not give way.

My silent dramatic farewells were of course premature and had to be quickly retracted. (Although had I had access to the Journals and seen the blackness of Marcus's mind I might have thought twice about retracting them and let them stand.) No sooner had I made them, in fact, than Marcia raised her head from her task – I saw now that she had been innocently sorting lentils like a good, thrifty housewife – spotted me at the window, and gave a smile of such radiance that my misgivings about her new personality melted away on the instant. Then she waved, pointing excitedly to someone in the room beyond me, and I turned to find that both Marcus and Commodus had now entered the hall, accompanied by I think it was Lucilla or one of the other girls, and were standing close by me, their arms held out in welcome, their faces also wearing what appeared to be large, uncontrived and perfectly happy smiles.

The meeting which I had so dreaded was therefore in fact an easy one, or one made easy, let us say, by tact and careful management. The aristocratic manner – that curious way which all the members of the Aurelii family had of cloaking their emotions, hiding their wounds and pretending that nothing untoward had happened to them nor ever could – does not come naturally to me, but I have lived long enough under its aegis to be impressed by it and to some extent conquered. My instinct would have been to have things out with Marcus immediately, to take him aside, tell him that I understood the reasons which had prompted his behaviour – *all* of them, the clear and the not-so-clear – and ask him quite simply where we stood, what he intended to do, and whether or not the Project was still alive. And the same with Commodus and Marcia: singly, perhaps, seeing that they were now best kept physically distant, but on impulse I would have taken them into my arms and encouraged them to talk, unburden themselves and tell me anything and everything that they wished. It is my physician's respect for fresh air, I suppose, for cleanliness and cathartics and drainage.

Set against the smiles of my two patrons, however, and the general air of grace and urbanity that they exuded, my instinct suddenly seemed a very poor and boorish thing to give rein to, and instead of following it, as I later realized I should have done, I allowed myself to fall into the seductive trap of feigning along with everyone else that all was well, that no violent deed had been committed, and that there were no wounds in need of medication. Marcus held me tightly to his chest, laid his cheek against mine and gave what I am almost sure was a sob and a fairly racking one at that, but when he stretched out his arms to examine my face for signs of change, the smile was firmly back in place. Linking us, yes, because the smile was genuine and affectionate, but also dividing us; erecting a kind of barrier between us on which was clearly marked, 'You may come so close, my friend, but beyond this point you shall no longer step.'

Commodus, too, when it was his turn to greet me, clung to me for a moment and then, like Marcus, stepped back to face me and pin me in place with a smile. But in his case I do not think this was done to distance me, merely to show me how our future relationship was best to be conducted. His father having set the tone, he was, so to speak, giving me a little demonstration of how we were to keep it up. Unlike his poor misunderstood head I have never doubted his guts, but if I had done, then his poise on this difficult occasion would have put me to shame. From the way he behaved he might just have won a lottery, not lost his childhood love to his sire in direct Greek-tragedy fashion.

A few moment later and Marcia herself joined us, skidding towards us across the floor in her exotic new slippers and inserting herself into the conversation with what seemed to me paramount ease – bowing to Marcus, kissing my hand, stroking Commodus's nose lightly but with great tenderness, and linking arms with her sister, or, I suppose one should say now, former sister – and the illusion of flawless reunion was complete.

Having once stepped into it, of course, the trap revealed itself increasingly difficult to escape from. If it had seemed boorish to accost Marcus on his arrival, it seemed downright barbaric to do so later, when he was properly installed again and things had begun to settle down. (And the lesson I learned from this must have been a sharp one, I think, for I remember the book in which I registered my failed experiments carried for this period the injunction to myself, written in large black letters, 'Remember: if you have questions to raise about anything, raise them fast.')

On the practical level, too, preparations for the founding of the Project went steadily ahead and I suppose this did much to set my mind at rest and foster in it the comforting illusion that no grave upset had really occurred. There were no more midnight talks between Marcus and myself and no more sharing of dreams, but masonry is more important than dreams, and one by one the bricks continued to be laid. Commodus was granted equal honours in the military triumph which marked his and Marcus's return. He was appointed Consul by special dispensation (he was still only fifteen) and a little later on, made Co-Emperor with his father. His marriage was celebrated to the wiry little Bruttia Crispina, and with this union much of his mother's money and much of his father-in-law's too passed into his hands. He was given (or more likely, I should think, purchased for himself) his own guard and independent living-quarters, where he held audience and – over a certain limited range of questions specially selected for him by his father – sat in judgement. In short, he became fully fledged Apprentice-Ruler, just as Marcus and I had always agreed that he should.

For my part I resumed my duties – at both courts, the major and the minor – tried to fit them in as best I could with a booming practice, and over the next eighteen months, which was roughly the period that elapsed before the next upheaval, went about my business as before.

Only once during this time did Marcus ever allude to the matter of Marcia's changed status with anything like sincerity, and this was on the day of the proclamation of Commodus's consulship, when, to tell the truth, we all of us drank a little too much wine and as a result became slipshod in our defences. He was lying beside me on a pile of cushions (an unusual fact in itself – that he be horizontal, I mean, and hostage to comfort) in Commodus's newly furnished and very pretty house, and was waving, if I remember rightly, in a rather over-dignified and owlish manner to the last of the departing guests (clerks and accountants most of them: the party had been for dependants), when suddenly, without any preamble, he turned towards me, grabbed me by the wrist, and staring me in the face with that hollow-eyed look I had seen on his face before, said, 'You know that I had to, Galen, don't you. And you know why I had to.'

Perhaps because we were both of us at roughly the same stage of tipsiness our minds were close, and despite the somewhat cryptic words I knew immediately what Marcus was referring to. I could tell too that he did not want from me a spoken reply. His eyes held mine for what seemed a long time, until he read the answer he was seeking. (And incidentally I hope it was what I intended; the face-language of courtiers was never my strong point.) Then he dropped my hand, forcefully, as if it had been holding his and not the contrary, and added, 'Leave me in peace, I beg of you. I have punishment enough as it is.'

A spare confession, but, as I say, in a year and a half of what for want of a better word I suppose I must call our renewed friendship, all I was to be granted. And it speaks so much for my fondness for Marcus when I confess that even in this minimal gesture, made under the influence of wine, was enough to draw me back to him again, or almost.

That I never completely reached him was, I think, chiefly due to the fact that any advance I made was rendered null by the speed of his own withdrawal. Although how far I was aware of this flight during Marcus's Roman stay, or if indeed I was aware of it at all, is something I am still, even now, unable to say for sure. All I know is that the barrier, which I at first saw as a simple device of Marcus's for keeping me at a distance, was in reality a far more complicated construction, designed to keep me at a fictive distance in order to prevent me from seeing how great the real distance between him and myself had already grown. I suppose you could say, then, that I was aware of *a* retreat on Marcus's part, but not *the* retreat.

Whether, and if so, how far, I ought to have been aware of what was happening – not as a friend this time but as the doctor in charge of treatment – is yet another matter. A more serious matter, I suppose, although I do not think of it that way myself, the loss of a friend seeming more grave to me than the loss of a patient.

I will take first the purely spiritual symptoms. Here, I think, I have little to reproach myself for: like the undermining of the Project, to which it was indeed closely connected, Marcus's canker, soul-rot, necrosis, or whatever one chooses to call it, was still heavily shrouded at this stage. It was in a very literal sense a closed book. He opened his mind to his Journals, that is, and he opened his Journals to no one but himself. I am familiar with the original manuscript, it is a holograph up to the last fourteen passages; and I know for a fact – because it was I who made the necessary arrangements – that even these last fourteen passages, composed when the author was no longer capable of holding a pen, were dictated to what is known as a 'tomb-scribe', i.e. to a man incapable of revealing to others the information in his possession. It was widely known *that* the Emperor was writing – the whole camp was made to keep silence sometimes while he did so – but nobody, not even Marcia who shared most of his thoughts by then, poor child, knew *what*, or in what ghastly tone. A good doctor treats the spirit with the rest of the man, and I pride myself on being quicker than most to spot intangible disorders such as lunacy and hydrophobia and the blight of the black bile; I diagnosed a case of frenzy once, for example, weeks before it exploded, from the extraordinary tidiness of the patient's surroundings – I could tell somehow, just by looking at the military precision of the chattels and the way they had been put into piles and lines and squares, that a cord within their owner's soul was about to snap. But when, as it was in Marcus's case, the malady is uncharted and is kept, moreover, a deep and deliberate secret by the sufferer himself, then even the best and most alert of therapists cannot, I think, blame himself for not having seen it sooner. On this account, therefore, I consider myself totally in the clear.

This ties up the spiritual symptoms. Let me turn now to the bodily ones. Was there, I ask myself, anything in Marcus's overt physical condition to which I ought, perhaps, have paid more attention? Anything – I do not know – which ought to have struck me as significant, as ominous, as either marking or heralding the inner decay?

It is a question I have naturally often put to myself before, and to which until now I have always given a very lenient answer. My deputy, after all, who was almost as good a clinician as I was myself, was quite happy about the health of his imperial charge during the years he served him. His reports, even those covering the long journeys homewards and the critical period of the Empress's illness and death, contained nothing that gave rise to worry – not on Marcus's account, that is. There had been rheums, bouts of insomnia and bouts of lethargy, several attacks of piles in correspondence with journeys, one or two superficial wounds, but otherwise little he seemed to think worthy of note. Two fevers, very quickly over. A cough two winters ago, not so swift to pass. Heartburn. Indigestion. Constipation. A touch now and then of the gripe. All the Emperor's usual complaints, in short, but apart from the piles which, judging from the description, had been bad, all of them unusually mild. Regarding medicines, no changes had needed to be made to my original prescriptions, and no other draughts had been administered save for the evening theriac in its usual proportions.

All very straightforward, then, all very reassuring. My own opinion, what is more, when I was able to form it, tallied perfectly with that of my assistant. I carried out a full examination shortly after Marcus's return, and although it was over six years now since I had seen him and these six years had been hard ones for him, to my surprise I found him fitter and stronger-looking than he was when he left. With, I confess, a thoroughness that I found strangely satisfying, I stripped him of his clothes – all of them, even his shift, and went over him like a slave-dealer at a fair; I stood him up, I laid him down, I turned him on one side, I turned him on the other; I flexed his joints, I pinched his tendons, I kneaded the liver, eavesdropped on the heart, sounded the lungs, smelt the breath, *tasted* the urine (for, as I point out here to an enthralled Cassius, merely sniffing at it is not enough), I fed his spittle to a frog, and the frog did not lose colour; I explored every inch of skin and every orifice – save for the anus which was still too sore to trouble – and came across no sign, no symptom which could possibly have been taken as indicative of the inner decay – unless one is to credit the facile theory which maintains there is a direct link between loss of body weight and loss of soul, doctrine which I myself believe to be nonsense. Marcus was thinner maybe, but no thinner than I'd seen him at other times.

This, anyway, is what I have always told myself. Just a few moments ago, however, as I was thinking back on what I described as the 'hollowness' of Marcus's eyes, and remembering how I was struck by this strange property of theirs on more than one occasion, it suddenly struck me that there probably *was* a sign, right there in the eyes, if I had only known how to read it. This hollowness, you understand, was not merely a look, an expression conveying sadness – although it was that also – but an actual physical phenomenon with an observable and apparently very simple cause. I had noticed the peculiarity before: it seemed to come and go, never interfering with the vision nor giving any trouble, and I had never really bothered much about it. But in the examination I now performed I noticed it far more clearly. Perhaps because it had meanwhile grown more pronounced, and perhaps also because I was looking more carefully and using lid-props and a candle: Marcus's eyes were literally losing their colour; like a beaten army, the green of the iris was shrinking, retreating, surrendering ground to the encroaching black of the pupil.

Could I, should I, I now ask myself, have inferred from this what any street-corner quack would probably tell you in a trice? Namely, that the eyes being the windows of the soul, when a man's eyes lose colour it means that his soul is losing colour behind them, and that when the eyes are prey to blackness it is in reality the soul which is being thus devoured? Sad to admit, because if so it is my science which is at fault seeing that it has taken me two decades to arrive at the quack's conclusion, but, in view of the gravity of the events that were shortly to take place, I think that I most definitely should have inferred just this.

'What should *I* infer, then, I would like to know?' says Cassius, who seems to have forgotten his packing and his visitors for the time being and since the reading of the Daybook has continued to sit beside me on an upturned case, his face so close to mine that I can smell his morning sardine on his breath. 'What should *I* infer, dear Doctor, from these secretive milky veils that cover your own eyes? That your soul has grown a case around it like a moth? That it hides itself? Dissembles? Does not reveal the whole truth?'

I had never expected of the Senator such acumen. I have no ready reply, and so let him continue while I try to think of one. Unchecked, his voice takes on more confidence.

'Am I to believe your stories, Galen, pray?' he goes on. 'And if so, when am I to believe them, and how many, and how far, and which parts? I know what you are going to tell me now. No, forgive me, what you are going to tell me later, because I can hear from the fuss the slaves are making that the first of my visitors has arrived. You are going to tell me that not only did Commodus put an end to the life of the divine and incomparable Marcus Aurelius – on your own rating the best and worthiest man that these sorry times of ours have ever produced – but that his action was right, necessary, perhaps even praiseworthy. That is what you are going to tell me unless I am very much mistaken. And in his defence you are going to offer me this peculiar argument about the connection between a person's eyes and a person's soul. Argument which it not only took you twenty years to think up, but, if sound, lands you and your screened, inscrutable soul in an extremely invidious position. You will, as the saying goes, unless you are very careful, find yourself impaled on your own stake.'

I will indeed. Perhaps I am already. Because hard as I try I can find no prompt rejoinder to Cassius's objection. The trouble is that I know it to be fundamentally right: I *have* concealed things from him, and shall continue to do so. This has little to do with the webs in my eyes, and a lot to do with the ruby-coloured spyglass he wears in his, but nevertheless I have not been entirely open in our dealings. I have exacted from him a maximum of honesty and have been given it, but on my side I have not been able to return the gift. What Marcus used to call the luxury of innocence has been denied me. In the interests of Truth I have had to use – not lies, fortunately, I have not had to stoop as low as that, but silences and screens and half-truths. And Cassius is right, my soul feels quite at home amongst them.

'I am flattered,' I manage to counter at last, 'that Your Excellency sees a strength where there is only weakness. Because the function of these webs of mine, alas, is not so much to prevent others from seeing in, as myself from seeing out. If my spirit is in the same plight as my body – so blind, so fumbling, so hindered in its movements, then surely there is little to fear from it. As regards the other objection, though, you are right, and I am bitterly ashamed. Your Excellency being so pressed for time and knowing already what I have to say, it was most thoughtless of me to crave this meeting. I have trespassed most brutally on your patience already. When you have reached your final decision – when you have decided that is, whether or not you believe my version of events and whether or not you find it worthy of recording – perhaps you would be so gracious as to inform me by letter. More than this I do not presume to ask.'

If anyone is impaled it is Cassius now, stuck by the rod of his own curiosity, but he takes his punishment laughing. 'You sly old fox, Galen,' he says. 'Why such humility all of a sudden? As far as I can see you presume on everyone and everything and your presumptions are usually correct. Kindly presume, therefore, that in spite of all my engagements you are invited to sup with me tomorrow evening to tell me the rest of your story. What do you say to that?'

In the event I say nothing, because with these words the Senator rises from the packing case and leaves me abruptly for his approaching guest. He too knows he can presume on my acceptance. But I am pleased and touched by his gesture, and turn up next evening half an hour early, a gift of special gout-balsam in my hand and the last instalment of my story ready on my tongue.

IN CAUDA VENENUM

(Poison in the end.)

A t the beginning of August, after a stay of eighteen months, Marcus and Commodus left Rome again for the battlefields of the north. They were travelling this time as far as the banks of the River Danube. I had been in the region myself with Marcus in the early days, before I took up my Court appointment and was still, so to speak, on approval with him as far as my doctoring was concerned, and had found the place dreary and inhospitable beyond my worst imaginings. For this and other reasons I begged leave to be excused from accompanying him on the present expedition, and Marcus, professing sorrow but, I think, secretly relieved to be free of me, granted my request.

As I had done, therefore, the morning of the last great exodus eight years earlier, but with none of my former glee, I stood at the gates among the other discarded servitors and watched the departure of the imperial train. Then, quicker this time than anyone else, not even waiting for the dung to fall on the paving stones, let alone cool, I strode off and went about my own affairs. They were, as I have already said, thriving and money-spinning as never before, and I had little time for brooding even if I had wanted to.

Over the next months I kept myself abreast of news via the normal channels. I received no personal messages – save for a polite treatise from Marcia about the language of certain barbarian tribes which I had asked her to make note of for me – and I expected none. Hopes for the Project were still alive in me, but I knew now, like a farmer does when he downs tools and battens himself in his hut with the beasts to withstand the winter, that this was a period of waiting; if I had sown well, then my crop sooner or later would come to fruition, if not, not; there was little else I could do about it. The cords of communication between my pupils and myself were at present inert, but I knew somehow that they were there whenever we should need them; not severed, not slack, not even particularly frayed.

It was not until December of the next year, however, a full seventeen months later, that these cords were set into operation. And with a considerable jerk. One morning, much to the consternation of my secretary Philostratus whose task it was to sit watch by the door and shoo away the many interlopers and would-be students, a horseman in civilian dress arrived at my school – gaunt, mud-spattered, dishevelled, like the parody of some Attic messenger in a poem, and barging his way past my poor human Cerberus as if he had been a lap-dog, broke in on me in mid-lesson and handed me a letter. I recognized the handwriting at once: it was from Commodus, and Commodus in none too steady a mood. Later, when I had time to notice it, I found it worrying, too, that he had not used the ordinary military post.

The message was terse: 'Commodus Antoninus to his friend and mentor, Galen: You are needed urgently. Come at once. Travel privately, and I will reimburse you on your arrival. Bring your warmest clothes and all of your drugs.'

I obeyed the instructions without delay, like a sheep-dog obeys a whistle and with just about the same amount of reflection. Pant, pant, pant, run, run, do this, do that, put this in here and that in there, and off. Had I taken longer I think my baggage could have been halved. In the days which followed, though, and particularly the nights, as I bowled and bounced my way northwards over mud and ice and stones, lying – as I always advised Marcus to do but which for reasons best known to himself he never would – in a cot suspended from the roof of the vehicle to avoid the worst of the shocks, I had plenty of time to study the slender text and try to squeeze from it a maximum of information.

Needless to say, I did not like what I extracted in the least. I did not like the slenderness itself for a start, which showed that the writer was under stress and worried about maintaining secrecy. I did not like the fact of Commodus's using a private courier, still less his insistence that I use one also: this seemed to indicate not only worry but downright fear. And I did not like the reference to medical ingredients either, because I had already been alerted by my assistant in his letters that a problem had arisen in this connection – to do with the theriac and its dosage and its efficiency – and began now to suspect that it was every bit as serious as he made out, and perhaps more so.

The journey, anyway, which fortunately I do not need to recall, took nine long days and eight long nights to complete, and I had if not the leisure then at least the time to think all these things over in my head as I clung to the sides of my cot, and swung and shook and shivered and wished myself earthborne.

Once again, though, as had happened before when I tried to envisage the possible dangers to the Project and wrongly thought that I had covered all of them, reality was to confound me. I was prepared for trouble with Marcus's health, trouble with the military, possibly a mix between the two, with Marcus ailing and losing his grip and the armies turbulent as a result; this was the sure if unoriginal conclusion that nine days' shaking had led me to. However, the problem, as it was put to me on my arrival by Commodus himself, who met my carriage on the outskirts of the camp, plucked me half-asleep from my cot with his own arms (no difficult feat for he had grown to twice my size by now) and drew me into a little out-of-the-way hut which I think he must have specially chosen for our meeting, appeared to be of a rather different nature. It concerned Marcus's health; it concerned military unrest also, and as a direct consequence, but it also had its curious and apparently irrelevant centre elsewhere.

A centre so strange and disconcerting that it took Commodus some time to reach it. He spoke slowly, haltingly, choosing his terms with an almost painful precision. Looking, I presume, for those which would enable him to reconcile loyalty to the truth with loyalty to his father; not always finding them. He had been wanting to send for me for many, many months now, he said, but had not done so because Marcus had been opposed to the idea. Marcus, in fact, had grown opposed to several ideas recently, but of this we would speak later. What he wanted me to understand now, however, was simply this, that he had respected his father's wishes – all of them, even those that had been hardest to follow and most directly in conflict with his own – for as long as he had continued to believe that they *were* his father's wishes. Thus, although he had longed for my presence more than the springtime, more than victory, more, almost, than the air he breathed, he had not sent the summons until now.

'And now?' I prompted gently. The mention of a change of ideas sent ice to my heart, but I did not want to interrupt and make Commodus's task more difficult than it already was: his last sentence had been further complicated by a visit from his old enemy the stutter.

Now, he said, now; well, now, he no longer believed that they were his father's wishes at all. Not in the sense that Marcus was no longer capable of having wishes and expressing them, I must understand: it wasn't that he had lost his awareness or lost the power of speech or volition or anything like that; perhaps it would have been better if he had. But in the sense that the person from whom the wishes came was no longer Marcus. I would see for myself all too soon what he meant by this, but to give me an idea of what to expect he would tell me of the last incident that had taken place – the one which had finally caused him to disobey Marcus's orders and send for me.

It was hard for him, though, Commodus went on after another long pause, to know how to set about describing exactly what had happened. Theft was a meaningless word to use in such connection – the Head of the Roman State owning as he did the entire contents of the world or nearly, he had only to ask for what he wanted and it was his, so to accuse his father of stealing was absurd before it was impious. Nevertheless, happenings had a life of their own independent of words, and the happening, the fact, or whatever you like to call it, was that a couple of weeks ago Marcus had been discovered by a slave – oh misery, how could he put it? Taking? Abstracting? Stealthily removing? Yes, perhaps that was the best term for it, stealthily removing by night certain medical goods from the camp supply. Like a slave himself. Like a chicken-thief or common pilferer.

You will see what I mean now about reality's power to confound. I was thunderstruck, robbed of words; robbed for a moment of my very reason. If I had been told that Marcus had turned into a twenty-pincered crayfish I could hardly have been more taken aback. Yet at the same time I knew immediately, as you do when somebody gives voice to a suspicion you have had for a long time but have so far refused to acknowledge, that what Commodus said was the truth. I do not believe in incubi that slip in through sleepers' nostrils at night and feed on their spirits; I do not believe in wolves that hide inside a man and pop out of him when the moon is high; I do not believe in ogres, or sirens, or harpies or indeed any of the members of that traditional predatory, soul-greedy fauna which populates the minds of the ignorant and disturbs their dreams, nor did I then. But I know that the spirit, like the body, has its enemies and its invaders – of a less fantastic cast than the imaginary, maybe, but every bit as ugly and every bit as dangerous. Thus I understood straight away, almost before Commodus had finished speaking and hours before I conducted my own examination, that the diagnosis he had made was correct, and that Marcus was indeed no longer Marcus, inasmuch as one or more of the above entities had penetrated his soul and made its nest there. And at a much earlier date, perhaps, than any of us realized.

When I think of this entity now, with the benefit of hindsight and bearing in mind in particular the detail of the gnawed irises which now seems to me so significant, I think of it not so much as a generic rot or decay as an individual living animal – a soul-worm or a soul-weevil; more likely the latter. Although unlike the majority of my colleagues, I realize that to put a name to a thing is not always to understand it, still less to have power over its workings.

In coining this name, I wish to be clearly understood, I am not bringing water to my own mill. Or not *only* to my own mill. Of course it suits me to maintain that it was the soul-weevil and not Marcus whom I argued with, wrestled with, pleaded with in vain in the following weeks. Of course I prefer to think that as I sat there within the stuffy confines of that tented world, discussing and defending the destiny of the real world outside, my opponent was not the man I revered above all others, nor even a man of any sort, come to that, but a foul worm-like creature which had usurped his body and now presented itself to me in his likeness. This is what I like to think, of course. And of course it is what I would like other people to think as well. But it is at the same time an exact description of the case. Or, again, as exact a description as I can ever hope to give.

Even without the knowledge that he had meanwhile turned, to use Commodus's blunt phrase, into a common pilferer or a chicken-thief, Marcus was truly unrecognizable. I visited him in his tent on the evening of that same day, after a long talk with my assistant and an even longer one with Marcia, and apart from the courtesy, of which there were still traces now and again in his behaviour, I found myself facing an almost total stranger. He was thinner than I had ever seen him, thinner than I had ever seen a living man.

(True, some of the consignments that used to be delivered to me from the mines contained bodies even more wasted, but these I do not count since they were dead.) His eyes were quite, quite black by now, the iris invisible, the skin of the face flushed and irritated, the nose runny, the mouth twisted from its former shape, and loose and chapped and, I think, uncomfortably dry as well, as he kept dabbing at it with a piece of damp cloth which he held in his hand for this purpose. The cloth was filthy, too – something the Marcus I knew would never have tolerated in the past.

As Commodus had predicted, he was conscious and knew perfectly well who I was, but was evidently very angry to see me there and did not allow me to touch him. For this reason I was unable to check the other symptoms which my assistant had warned me to look out for such as the shallow breathing, the decreased body temperature, the lazy pulse and so forth. I noticed, however (it would have been hard not to), the gooseflesh and the shudders and the lack of control over the limbs – particularly the right foot, which, just as my assistant said, now and again shot out in a kicking movement like a donkey's hoof. You had to be quite careful if you were standing nearby not to be struck by it.

It was terrible, terrible to see a man you had once loved and admired reduced to such a state. And it was even more terrible to be able to do so little to assist him. I mocked Cassius earlier for thinking that paradoxes are evil things – a paradox, after all, is just a figure of speech, a knot you tie with words, and as such can hardly be said to possess a moral connotation; but all the same I am bound to admit that the physician's paradox in which my assistant and I now found ourselves floundering had something distinctly evil-flavoured about it.

Our dilemma briefly was this: we both of us knew without a doubt that Marcus in his midnight raid on the camp medical chest had been after poppy juice: soothing and sleep-inducing extract which normally formed a staple ingredient of his evening theriac, but which recently had been deliberately removed from the brew on my instructions precisely because it was so soothing and sleep-inducing. This was the course we had always adopted in the past: whenever, as I confess sometimes happened, Marcus got over-drowsy and fell asleep during audience or some other important meeting, we would simply cut down on the poppy juice or eliminate it altogether until he was brighter, and it was the course we had adopted now. My assistant had written that his patient was becoming dull and irritable and sleepy; I had written back instructions, and the extract had been suspended. *With*, I may add, as in the past, Marcus's full consent.

Why, as Commodus so reasonably pointed out, a man in the Emperor's position should then have resorted to the base act of stealing, when all he had to do was to call for my assistant, tell him he had changed his mind, and order him to put the missing ingredient back in the theriac again, puzzled both my assistant and myself deeply. (And continued to puzzle me for years: indeed it is only thanks to the notion of the soul-weevil and its insidious gnawing of the moral fibres that I begin to understand it now.) But we could see why it was that part of Marcus's nature wanted the poppy extract and part did not, because that was exactly what we felt about it ourselves. On the one hand, that is, we could see that certain of the symptoms we were trying to eliminate, such as the drowsiness and languidity, were caused directly *by* it, and on the other hand we could also see, more and more clearly as the weeks went by, that certain other of the symptoms could not be cured *without* it.

I do not want to relive the various phases of our struggle in detail, not even to justify myself with Cassius. It lasted ninety interminable days, and even now the memory of them is too bitter to stomach, even now the tentacles of the nightmare are ready to catch at me and drag me down. I do not ever wish to see again, not even with the eye of my mind, the board with its straps, or the gag with its saliva, or the fits, or the trembling, or the vomiting, or the grimaces; I do not want to remember the rages, when it would seem the tent was about to fall down about our ears, so fiercely did Marcus resist us, or the days of listlessness and inertia when he would lie still and cold and dry like a lizard in winter and make no move at all. I do not want to remember the way he clung to me like a child, or struck out at me like an enemy, or the way he would call for Marcia to warm him and make her lie down beside him on the board for hours and cry into her hair. No, I do not want to remember any of this.

We tried, I think it is fair to say, every remedy we had at our disposal, working our way through the entire alphabet of our drugs from infusions of aconite to ochre plasters. We tried forcibly suspending the poppy extract, we tried replacing it by infusions of mallow and camomile, we tried administering it at irregular intervals, we tried administering it at regular intervals. Then when none of these methods gave results we tried ignoring the contradiction altogether, and simply went ahead and administered more and more of the extract until we could no longer bear the smell or the sight of it. All to no avail – the symptoms would not cease. I suppose because by then it was too late and the weevil had already wreaked its damage. The thinness became skeletal, the nose continued to run, the pupils to gape, the skin to itch; the fits of shaking became more frequent, degenerating now to authentic seizures; and sleep when it came was shallow and troubled and did little to restore.

And if these the physical ravages of the parasite were devastating, the spiritual were worse: not by chance do I identify the creature as a soul-weevil. The last pages of Marcus's Journals which he composed at this time, crouched in his foetal position with the wretched tomb-scribe squatting on the ground beside him trying to catch the gist of the hastily murmured words, give a very clear picture of the extent of the damage. In them you can see, trapped and frozen there like insects in ice, all the disgust, the loathing, the disenchantment that their author felt for the things of this world which had once been dear to him. You can taste the sourness of his humours, feel the tiredness of his limbs, see the darkness of his mind and, if you are equal to the journey, even sink with him into the abyss that he then inhabited and visit it first-hand. (I repeat, I think myself that the result is art, and art of quite an extraordinary intensity and quality, but that is an aesthetic consideration which I keep separate from the others. No one else agrees with it anyway.)

I did not, as I said, have access to these Journals when Marcus was alive, and I had quite some difficulty in gaining it after his death: they were thought to contain his political testament and there was a great deal of scuffling and squabbling before I was able to lay my hands on them. But to the ends of gauging his inner ruin I scarcely needed them. My patron and one-time friend may have hidden his thoughts from me, but he could scarcely hide the mind from which they had sprung. Or crawled would be the better word, the thoughts had become so slow and feeble.

Again, the memory is one I hardly care to look back on. We had, Marcus and I, many long conversations together in this three-month period of time, and many long and bitter arguments as well. Once he had got over his initial displeasure at seeing me and our doctor-patient relationship was back on more or less its old footing, he would call for me – usually in the morning when his brain was fresher, but sometimes in the afternoons and sometimes late at night – and ask me to talk to him. Or else, if he was capable of doing so, talk to me himself. Quite why he desired these meetings I do not know because he had long since stopped drawing pleasure from my company, and certainly it was not the moral justification of his political change of heart that interested him. Most likely, I suppose, they simply served to help him pass the time.

The greater part of what he said is blurred now, inasmuch as it was badly blurred already when he said it and my failing memory has done the rest. Some things, however, landmarks or, should I say, tidemarks of the flood of his despair, still stand out clearly. Not once, so far as I can remember, did he retract explicitly; nowhere did he condemn the Project, in no precise spot or at no precise moment did he bury the corpse of it before my eyes and trample on its grave; he merely threw earth on it, spadeful after spadeful in an attempt to stifle. Here are some of the sayings I best recall:

'The government of men is a murderer's task, Galen. I want my son to be relieved of it, to have no blood on his hands. Look at mine, look at mine, how they drip, how they reek!'

'There is no such thing as a good form of government: salvation is not for the many, it cannot be bestowed or engineered; it is to be sought by the individual, and where he or she seeks it and in what condition is of no matter.'

'The only just actions a man can perform are negative ones: never to hurt, never to judge, never to presume.'

'Never to hurt, Galen, remember that. Not even in the name of Wisdom, not even in the name of Mercy.'

The turn his thoughts had taken is not difficult to see: he had lost faith in mankind and its destiny, lost hope, lost sympathy and one might almost say lost interest as well. The blood on his hands was a subject he returned to often. In the throes of his heavier fits he seemed actually to see it, and would rub his hands on the bed-covers, rhythmically, frantically, at length, as if trying to remove the stains. I think I have mentioned, too, the time I found him contemplating an ant with such infinite and misplaced tenderness, and of how he used its wobbly progress across his palm to try to make me understand that morality as he saw it could only be measured in similarly minute and tentative terms. (I *did* understand all too well; I most strongly did not agree.) But most revealing of all was perhaps another saying of his, again concerning forms of government and the structuring of power, the last part of which he repeated more and more frequently towards the end until it became a kind of chant or dirge. It was this:

> 'The aim of such a structure, Galen, must never, as we thought, be that of enabling a good man to do good, but on the contrary that of preventing bad men from doing evil. Understand that and you will have understood all that philosophy is able to teach on the subject. Forget Plato, forget the Vision of Good, concentrate on the Vision of Evil and try to foil it – everywhere, in every place, at every time.'

This, then, in all its nightmarish complexity was the situation that Commodus and I were faced with, and this the context in which we were called to act. Our motives? Well, motives are always difficult things to ascertain. Even if you dissect them and hold them up to the light you are liable to find a kind of resident opacity and viscousness, a clinging together and interdependence of the fibres that makes it impossible to say what substance they are really made of. It is rather like the question of the stars. Did Marcus's change of heart regarding the Project determine Commodus's and my final decision, or did it influence it, or did it do neither, or did it do both? And if it determined, how strongly did it determine? And if it influenced, how far did it influence and in what way? Negatively? Positively? Formatively? Just to begin with? Right up to the end?

And the fact that the Quintilian brothers were summoned to the Emperor's tent more and more often in the last weeks and were entrusted with more and more powers, what role did this play? Did it lend force to our decision, or merely add haste to it, or did it have nothing to do with it at all? Were we in part *caused* to do what we did by the talk which now began to circulate in the camp, regarding a resurgence of the Republic, or were we spurred, or what?

These are questions I prefer not to answer, prefer hardly to pose. Of course Commodus desired leadership, his entire education to date had been centered on nothing else – the acceptance and rightful management of a political power that would one day be his. Of course he desired Marcia also, just as Marcia desired him. And of course I myself desired above all things to save the Project from Marcus's stranglehold and bring it out into the light; even if this meant, in terms of midwifery, ripping open the womb that had conceived it and sacrificing the life of the parent for that of the child. We were rational beings all of us, of course these considerations carried weight with us, it would be absurd to pretend that they did not. But accompanying these desires maybe and yet at the same time totally eclipsing them in terms of strength and urgency was another: namely, that an end be put to Marcus's suffering, a limit set to his debasement. We could not, to put it briefly, bear to stand by and watch his ruin any longer.

No doubt Cassius's curiosity craves the minutiae of what actually took place that evening when I crept unseen into Marcus's tent and thwarted the weevil once and for all of its prey, but again I must disappoint him. Not out of cowardice this time, but because the memory is gone of its own accord. Some things, like the outbursts of volcanoes, are so violent that they leave no mark – merely a soft grey blanket that covers everything. And then, what is there to be told? There was no real plan, no plotting, no consultation. Never once did Commodus and I discuss together what was to be done, or look one another in the eye and agree silently, 'Now. Now, before it is too late.' When things are necessary they happen – in their own way, in their own time. Marcus's agony could not continue and it did not continue. I know that I cannot have used mushrooms because it was not the season, but I know that I used something just as effective. And I know that when I had used it, and saw the dark foreign eyes cloud over, and the shaking limbs relax, and the poor tormented frame achieve stillness, I felt still and peaceful myself for the first time since my arrival at the camp.

I have a faint recollection of Marcia being there as well – asleep perhaps, because it had become her habit to take snatches of sleep while she could, curled up at Marcus's feet like a watchdog – and of my somewhat foolishly waking her and telling her that it was over and to go on sleeping. I may even have said something about the setting of the old sun and the rising of a new one on the morrow. To comfort her, you understand. But the soft grey blanket is mercifully thick, and of this I cannot be sure. All that stays with me is the sense of absolute peace and absolute rightness that I felt on looking down on my handiwork: when a physician quenches pain he is indeed, as my old chemistry teacher used to say, doing the work of a god.

PART IV

THE HISTORIAN'S VERDICT

LUX VERITATIS

(Cicero's optimistic definition of history: a light
which illuminates the truth.)

C hickens are luckily not nocturnal birds, and memories apart, my
supper with Cassius has been a strangely pleasant and restful
affair, even if it has taken place, like most other things in the Senator's
household, outside in the favoured courtyard. The food was good, as
I knew it would be, the couches are comfortable, the night is mild,
the service a little slap-happy but discreet. When I have finished my
story we sit in silence, each of us busy with our thoughts, from the
sound of it the Senator busy with a toothpick as well.

Despite the meal, which was large, I feel emptied, relaxed. Not
like a victor, but like a combatant, possibly vanquished, who has put
his all in the fight and has nothing to reproach himself for. A hardy
old acorn. Let Severus have his way, let his lies prevail, let the crushing
judgement on my Philosopher-Prince echo down the centuries; more
than this, I tell myself, I cannot do.

Nevertheless, unlike the poor acorns who know all too well what
the future holds for them, I cannot help feeling a certain amount
of anxiety about my fate. Or let us say the fate of this precious
bundle of information that I have laid like a trusting hunting-dog at
Cassius's feet to do with as he pleases. And when the silence becomes
too long I begin to make small noises of encouragement, clearing
my throat and gently tapping my blind-man's stick up and down on
the floor.

The Senator responds by more vigorous tooth cleansing, and then I
hear a crackle of papers. True to character he has prepared notes for his
reply. Once again whether this promises ill or well for the destiny of
my stories I cannot say, but I presume it means that he has at least paid
both them and me the courtesy of careful reflection. His voice – and
this does *not* bode well – when it comes contains a note of strain.

Cassius has followed this extraordinary tale of mine, he says, with interest and, almost despite himself, with a growing sense of conviction. I am not to be offended by this, but at the outset I appeared to him like a man with a sackful of goats' turd, bent on trying to persuade a customer that what he has to offer is in fact not goats' turd at all but a heap of priceless black pearls. That is how desperate and preposterous my undertaking seemed to him. With each item that came out of the sack, however, his certainties about its nature dwindled, and now that the sack is empty of all its contents spread out here before him in a row he tends to think that my claim was an honest one and that despite their grubby and unpromising appearance my wares are indeed what I said they were: pearls. Of a kind.

One or two of these pearls, mind you, he continues in that taut, rather edgy voice I find so unsettling, have a fairly nasty dung-like smell clinging to them and are sticky to the touch and softer then they should be and cause him still a certain amount of doubt, but he will list for me those which he is now prepared to accept as genuine. We will follow, if I do not mind, the order of his original notes, so that we can be sure that nothing is missing. Although we will compress a little:

CONCEPTION, BIRTH, INFANCY AND CHILDHOOD:
Commodus was no by-blow of a reprobate gladiator but the rightful son and heir of the great and wise Emperor Marcus Aurelius, whom he closely resembled and not only in the flesh but in character and disposition as well. Despite the purity of his parentage the child was born with three defects – a stutter, an inguinal rupture, and a tendency towards left-handedness; none of which defects, however, in the eyes of science carries the shameful moral stigma that is popularly alleged. In every other respect, body, soul and temperament, he was a perfectly normal boy, showed normal tastes, normal or perhaps we might even say higher than normal abilities, and led a perfectly ordinary life. His breath was sweet, he cast an everyday greyish shadow which like all shadows turned darker in full sunlight, he had a temper but he learnt how to control it. At the age of nine, on the death of his second brother, he became his father's sole heir and was handed over to me, Galen of Pergamos, in the conviction, as then shared by both Marcus Aurelius and myself, that I could make of him the ideal Platonic ruler.

A pause here while the Senator readjusts his papers. I loosen my hold on my stick, which I find I am gripping tightly as if it were a weapon:

I can hardly believe it possible that things should be going so well. He continues:

YOUTH: Again, a period of normal development and growth, marred only by an unfortunately strong attachment on the part of Commodus to his adopted sister Marcia Aurelia. The girl, however, was later dis-adopted, becoming first concubine to Marcus, and then, on Marcus's death, concubine to Commodus himself. The charge of incest between brother and sister is therefore not entirely unfounded but badly exaggerated. (And with regard to this young woman, Cassius adds, after all the things I have told him he is prepared to take back what he said about her being coarse and low-born and vulgar to look at, but he still clings to his opinion that she was tall, because she was.)

MATURITY: The events of this later period are all to be seen, or in most cases *re*-seen, in the context of the curious quasi-Platonic attempt at political architecture referred to above, and the not-so-curious attempts on the part of others, unsympathetic to the new style of building, to destroy it. Commodus was neither mad, nor vicious nor vindictive, but it was essential to his policy that the senatorial and moneyed classes be deprived of their power and riches and in some cases their lives, and this he steadily and systematically set about doing. Thereby (forgive him for putting it so simply, Cassius says, but this is the essence of the case as he now understands it) incurring the bitter hatred of both these categories. The young Emperor taxed, fined, confiscated, diminished the powers of the Senate, slighted its members, promoted commoners in their stead, did everything he could to concentrate power into his own hands; and the senators and landowners responded by just as steadily and systematically vilifying him in the eyes of his peers; until fairly predictably one of them stepped in and put an end to things. Commodus did not, as was alleged, murder people wholesale out of spite; he suppressed one serious conspiracy against his rule, and that in as economical a way as possible. He did not keep a private brothel with six hundred inmates, he did not torture people personally for the fun of it, still less did he debauch virgins of both sexes as a stable pastime – these things are all false charges brought against him by an angry and resentful Senate. His oratory was not good, but his speeches were not the ludicrous

175

affairs they were made out to have been. His disturbance of the rites of certain religious cults was not due to impiety, but had a reason behind it. And last but most important of all, his exhibitions in the arena, questionable though they may have been from the point of view of taste, were not performed out of vanity or folly or blood lust, but again formed part of a calculated attempt to bypass the Senate and to show the common people that their welfare did not depend on intermediaries but derived directly from the Emperor's own person. Still for reasons tied up with this policy no doubt, but he *did*, however, dye his hair and wear very strange clothes and practise some very odd habits.

Cassius lays aside his notes and draws a deep, deep sigh. I notice that I am once more clinging on to my stick with unnecessary force and hurting my hands in the process.

'Your Excellency really believes all these things now?' I ask, loosening my fingers and trying to keep my voice as calm and neutral as I can. 'You are convinced of the truth of all that you have just said?'

'I do,' Cassius replies. 'I am. You underestimate me, Galen, I am not such an innocent as I seem. As I said, I have certain reservations. For example, I know that you have concealed things from me, but I am ready to accept without question that they are things of no great historical importance. You know how curious I am about most things, but I assure you in this case I do not even want to know what they are. Another point I am not entirely happy about, and that is your account of the death of Marcus Aurelius. It leaves me wondering a little. A Roman Emperor, any Roman citizen come to that, is not a rabbit or a weasel that you can hit him over the head with a club to put him out of his misery – no matter how great his suffering. Is this normally your way with patients? If so, I hope I am never in your care when I am really poorly. But I do not think that this *is* your way. No, I think that, as you said yourself, your motives were mixed and you did not care to examine them closely, but if you had done so I suspect you might very likely have found mercy in second place and political ambition, philosophical ambition, or whatever you like to call it, in the first.'

I make to protest at this sneaking piece of injustice but Cassius overrides me. 'And there is also,' he says, 'the question of

Commodus's part in the affair. Admittedly he had you, his physician, to advise him and do all the dirty work, but even so the act he shared in is by far the gravest that a man can ever commit. Would *I* have had the courage to sanction the killing of my own father, I ask myself, even if I had seen him in the state that you describe – abject, suffering, prey to a horrible inner parasite? I wonder. I rather hope I would not. However,' he continues, 'none of these things interfere with my basic judgement on your story, Galen. With gaps maybe and one or two dark patches, but I think your version of events is indeed the true one.'

This time I can no longer keep my voice in check and it comes out squeaky with excitement like that of a child. 'They are safe with you then, Excellency, my stories? You will take care of them, record them, pass them on?'

There is a moment's silence. 'I will take care of them, Galen,' comes the crushing reply, 'in so far as I will remember them and continue to acknowledge them in my mind as the truth. I will *not*, however, record them. Neither now when it would be foolhardy to do so, nor later when perhaps it will be safe. You will want to know my reasons for this and I will tell you them, but first be so good as to tell me something. What would have happened if Severus had failed in his overthrow and the Project had reached conclusion? What complexion would our State wear today? You say that Commodus on his concubine's recommendation had chosen as the mainstay, the architrave, or whatever you like to call it, of his policy the Jewish or Christian religion. Does this mean he would have proclaimed himself a god in his lifetime, and that we would all of us had to bow down before him and offer sacrifice?'

'I think not, Excellency, if that is what troubles you,' I reply. 'The Christians are secretive about their gods and only have one of them anyway. As I remember, the plan was merely that Commodus be appointed leader of the faithful on earth. Their Chief-Priest, Overseer, or Bishop as I think he is called.'

'Ah,' says Cassius. 'Nevertheless, we would all of us have been obliged to abandon the faith of our ancestors and adhere to the new cult whether we liked it or not?'

'Encouraged, Excellency,' I correct him. 'That is perhaps the better word. All members of the population would have been encouraged to accept the Christian creed. And it was, as I said, Commodus's conviction that most of them *would* like it in the end, or come to like it. Many of them – far, far more than your Excellency would imagine – already did.'

Cassius is silent for a moment. 'I see,' he murmurs. 'And so that was why Severus has had to go to such lengths to cover all the traces, was it? Because the followers were so numerous, and the attempt so nearly succeeded? Not because things were going badly, but because they were going all too well. I see, I see.'

He heaves another sigh and makes a great fuss with his papers; either consulting them or, what is more likely, putting them aside. 'Yes, yes,' he says, 'it all ties in, it all makes sense. And that is why you, Galen, on your side, are so anxious that the traces remain. I see it all now, I understand, I believe, I can even to some extent sympathize, but still my answer remains no. I do not think that any good can come about by making these things public. There are senses, you understand, in which black pearls can be fouler and more offensive than goats' dung. You have achieved your end, convinced me, won me round, given me new eyes, new ears, opened up whole new vistas on a landscape which I never imagined existed, but you still have not convinced me that what I have seen is beautiful. Let alone worthy of being shown to others.'

I bow my head in resignation. I would be quite willing to ignore the reasons behind Cassius's refusal now I know that it is a refusal, but this is not to be allowed. 'The idea of a State without a Senate', he goes on, his voice shedding its embarrassment and becoming firmer and louder with every word, 'is repugnant to me. Not because I am a senator myself, but because I believe that the Senate is a fine institution necessary to good government. Or perhaps as Marcus Aurelius in the grip of his weevil would have said, necessary to prevent bad government. The idea of a State in which everyone but the Emperor is equally powerless and equally poor, I also find disgusting – and again not only because I happen to have money and a position to defend, but because it seems to me a thing against Nature. And as far as the Christian religion is concerned, and the thought of being, as you put it, 'encouraged' to belong to it, with its revolting teachings of dead bodies emerging from their graves and bread turning into flesh and wine to blood and whatnot, this fills me not so much with disgust as with absolute dread.'

Having reached shouting pitch almost with his last sentence,

Cassius stops and takes up again on a quieter note. 'I am not a very clever man, Galen, and I am not very public-spirited. Marcus Aurelius was clever and public-spirited (or was until the weevil got him); Commodus, I am sure of this now, was clever and public-spirited, and you are clever and public-spirited yourself. All three of you have the edge over me in both these respects, and yet I think I could have come up with a far, far better world than the one you had in mind to build. Merely because I would have lacked the brain and the heart to build at all, but would have limited myself to adding little patches and improvements to this one. I would have been a mason, not an architect; a cobbler, not a shoemaker; a mender, not a creator. In Commodus's position, during the Sea-Battle I would have sent regular fighters into the arena with or without their fish-tails; I would have kept well clear of crypts; I would have crushed the conspiracy much as he did perhaps, but I would have been politer to my senators and would never have brandished ostrich heads at them. And I would not, no, I am certain of this now, I would not have done away with my own father merely because with half his brain gone and less cleverness and less concern for others to obscure his political visions he had begun to see the doctrines of Plato for what they were: a pack of dangerous, high-minded nonsense.'

So there it is at last. A long and implacable verdict against which there is no appeal. Despite these weeks of effort and these torrents of words and all his recent assurances to the contrary, the Senator's mind remains much as it was at the start, narrow, foreign, partisan and totally unreceptive. His eloquence surprises me a little – I did not know he could string so many words together without tripping over them, but his ideas and the verdict itself do not. There is little can be said to a man who candidly professes disinterest in the destiny of his fellow men. Cobbler indeed! There is no place for cobblers in statecraft. In statecraft to cobble is to botch; to patch is to bungle; to add bricks to an already shaky structure is to bring it to the ground. His last remark about Marcus 'seeing through' the Platonic doctrines is so utterly and grossly wrong that I ought not to let it pass: the weevil did not sharpen Marcus's vision, it destroyed it all together, as it destroyed the rest of him. But I remind myself of Marcus's own tolerance and say nothing.

I remember Marcus's manners as well, and before taking my

leave am careful to thank His Excellency as warmly as I can under the circumstances for all the time and attention that he has given me. These are not the words I use, but his patience has been almost as great as mine and his reward as meagre. I find to my surprise that I have grown quite fond of the little man, and my wishes for his health and his career are sincere, even though neither are of particular use to me any more.

I pause for an instant on the threshold as my slave fumbles with the lamp and throw one last little shaft. 'Not all the truth then, Excellency,' I say, 'not even much of it. But could you not include just enough of it in your works so that someone else can discern it? One day, I mean, in some distant future?'

It may be cowardly of me but I do not wait for the reply.